Penguin Books
Big man

Ed McBain is the pseudonym of Evan Hunter, one of America's most distinguished novelists. He was born and grew up in New York City, from where he takes the background of his 87th Precinct stories. After war service in the U.S. Navy, he attended Hunter College, moving from there through teaching and work for a literary agency to become the full-time professional writer he is today. As Ed McBain he has published forty 87th Precinct mysteries and the exploits of his gritty police team led by Detective Steve Carella have sold massively world-wide. When asked how he writes an 87th Precinct novel, he said, 'I usually start with a corpse. I then ask myself how the corpse got to be that way, and I try to find out – just as the cops would . . . I believe strongly in the long arm of coincidence because I know cops well, I know how much it contributes to the solving of real police cases. I'll use it unashamedly whenever I choose because I don't believe in mystery-writing rules. A mystery should be exciting, believable, and entertaining.' He has also written many novels under his real name including the best-selling *Blackboard Jungle* which was also made into a successful film starring Glenn Ford and Sidney Poitier. Many of his novels are published in Penguins, including *Cop Hater*, *Death of a Nurse*, *Lady Killer*, *The Mugger* and *Killer's Payoff*.

Big Man

Ed McBain

*(Originally published under
the pseudonym Richard Marsten)*

Penguin Books

Penguin Books Ltd, Harmondsworth, Middlesex, England
Viking Penguin Inc., 40 West 23rd Street, New York, New York 10010, U.S.A.
Penguin Books Australia Ltd, Ringwood, Victoria, Australia
Penguin Books Canada Limited, 2801 John Street, Markham, Ontario, Canada L3R 1B4
Penguin Books (N.Z.) Ltd, 182–190 Wairau Road, Auckland 10, New Zealand

First published in the U.S.A. in 1959
First published in Great Britain by Penguin Books 1978
Reprinted 1979, 1985, 1987

This is a work of fiction. The people and the
incidents were all invented by the author.

Printed and bound in Great Britain by
Cox & Wyman Ltd, Reading
Set in Intertype Times

This is for Norman
and Eudice

1

It was Jobbo first told me about the car snatches.

I never liked Jobbo, not even when we were snotnosed kids together, and I didn't like him that night either – but sometimes he made sense. Besides, it was one of those crazy summer nights where the heat hangs over you like a wet blanket, and even the buildings seem to be dripping a sooty kind of sweat.

I don't know if you ever been in New York to live. I don't mean to visit because then you get the tourist jive, and you figure the city is all Broadway lights and Fifth Avenue department stores. It ain't. And you can never feel the city like in the summertime when you can hear all the noises and when every guy and his brother is out in the streets trying to get a breath of air because it's so damn hot in the apartment you could choke. On nights like those, you don't even feel like breathing. You go downstairs and you lounge around outside the candy store and you watch the girls go by, like in the song. Anyway, that's what we were doing that night.

I remember the paper truck came by and dropped the newspapers on the sidewalk, and Jobbo walked over with the corded bundle and pulled a copy out, handing it to me. Then he carried the bundle inside to Mike who owned the candy store. It was just a little dumpy store and if you didn't know Mike was also a numbers collector, you would have wondered how come he could make a living in this ratty little joint. When Jobbo came out again, I was looking through the paper.

'What do you see, Frankie?' he asked.

'The usual jive,' I said. 'They're talkin' now about sendin' a rocket to the moon.' I folded the paper. 'You want this?'

'Too hot to read,' Jobbo said.

'Yeah.'

Jobbo was a fat guy who sweated a lot. He never wiped the sweat away. I think that son of a bitch *liked* to sweat. He just let it roll down his face and his neck, and then his T-shirt sort of sopped it up so that there was always a big wet ring around his chest and armpits. He also stunk a lot. To tell you the truth, he was a pretty disgusting animal. But he was one of these guys who got insulted if you told him he should take a bath. His last name was Giamboglio, but nobody wanted to get tangled in a handle like that one, so everybody called him Jobbo.

'What do you do on a night like this, Frankie?' he asked me.

'You croak from the heat.'

He nodded a little, sweating and smiling and stinking. Then he thought a while. When a fat guy thinks, you can almost hear the wheels going around inside his skull. Then he said, 'How come you ain't with what's-her-name?'

'Who do you mean?' I said.

'May.'

'Who says I got to be with her every night?'

'Well, what I mean, you been with her a lot lately.'

'I took her out a couple of times, so what? Does that make us engaged?'

'I didn't say you was engaged,' Jobbo said. 'Listen, man, if you're gettin' some of that stuff, it's fine with – '

'You don't know what you're talking about,' I said. 'She's a good kid.'

'Sure.'

'Well, she is. So let's drop the subject. I ain't with her tonight because I don't feel like being with her. There's no damn strings on me, mister.'

'No,' Jobbo said, and I didn't like the way he said it.

'Look, Jobbo, leave me be,' I told him. 'I was standing here taking it easy and you come over with your crap, and nobody invited you. So just do me a favor, and shut up.'

'Sure,' Jobbo said. He was quiet for a long time, but I could hear those wheels going around in his head, clickety-click, clickety-click. 'On a night like this,' he said, 'if a guy has nothing else to do – '

'On a night like this, I like to just not move, Jobbo. You move on a night like this, and you drown in your own sweat.'

'Sure, sure. But on a night like this, a smart boy knows what to do. Now you're a smart boy, Frankie.'

'I am, huh?'

'Damn right you are. Now what does a smart boy do on a night like this?'

'You tell me, Jobbo.'

'Well, a smart boy don't stand around and sweat on a night like this. Not when he can be doing other things.'

'You want to go over to the Jefferson pool? That it?'

Jobbo shook his head. 'I'll tell you something, Frankie. On a night like this, a lot of people go driving in their cars.'

'So what?'

'So it's hot, they roll the windows down. They park the car, and sometimes they forget to roll the windows up again. You follow me, Frankie?' His voice had dropped to a whisper. I had to lean close to hear him, and the stink was powerful close up.

'People leave things in cars, Frankie. Radios, purses, coats, lots of things. You follow me?'

'I'm not interested,' I said.

'Okay,' Jobbo said. 'Forget I mentioned it.'

We leaned against the stand and watched the chicks. In the summertime you really get an eyeful when they parade. They wear only these light silk dresses with hardly anything underneath, and when it's really hot the silk sticks to their bodies. I think I'd rather watch chicks walking in the summer than do just about anything else in the world.

'Suppose the cops show?' I asked Jobbo.

'Look, forget I mentioned it, will you? You're not interested, all right you're not. That's all she wrote.'

'Don't go hip on me, Jobbo. I asked you a question.'

'You can do lots of things if the cops show,' Jobbo said, his voice dropping again.

'Like what?'

'You can run.'

'And get shot in the back?'

'You ever hear of anybody getting shot around here? Man, that's all rumors,' Jobbo said.

'Pasco got shot,' I said, 'and that wasn't no rumor. If it was a rumor, it bled all the way down his leg.'

'Oh, sure, the leg maybe,' Jobbo said. He turned his attention to one of the chicks walking by. 'Man, look at that,' he said. He licked his lips and then said, 'Getting shot in the leg ain't nothing, believe me. What's a little hole in the leg?'

'*You* got a hole in the *head!*' I said.

'Besides, you don't have to run from the Law. There are other ways. You can just pile right into the car, just like it's your own heap. You make like you're fiddling with the ignition or something until the Snow White cruises on. That's all.'

'And the cops are gonna buy that, huh? The cops are gonna buy a sad story like that, huh? Jobbo, you got *two* holes in the head.'

'Okay, then skip it,' Jobbo said. 'I asked you, and you said no, so let's skip it.'

'You ever done this before?'

'Lots of times.'

'Where do you ditch the stuff?'

'I got connections.'

'Sure, you're a big man.'

'I ain't a big man, not yet I ain't, but I got connections.'

'What does a radio bring you?'

'Five, usually, if it ain't an *old* portable. You be surprised how many people leave portables in their cars.'

'And a coat, how about that?'

'Depends on what kind of coat it is. You get more for the fur jobs.'

'Who's gonna wear fur in this heat?'

'You be surprised, Frankie. When a dame's got a mink, she wears it even in Hell.'

'It sounds risky,' I said.

'For a jerk, yeah. But for a couple of down cats, it's duck soup.'

'And we're just a couple of down cats, huh, Jobbo?'

Jobbo grinned, his big round face splitting over yellow teeth.

10

'Frankie,' he said, 'in every crowd there's a smart boy.' He paused. 'In this crowd, there's *two* of them.'

We hit the East River Drive first.

I still didn't know why I was going along with Jobbo, except it sounded like kicks, and there's nothing can be so draggy as a hot summer night. Besides, it was nice and cool by the river, and it didn't smell so bad tonight like it sometimes did. They dump the whole city into the East River and, boy, sometimes it gets unbearable. I used to swim in there when I was a kid, before I learned about how polluted the water was. Sometimes that Jefferson pool gets so crowded you could drown and your own mother standing next to you wouldn't know you went under. So I used to go down to the river instead. Until I learned it was polluted and you could get every disease including the African Crud from swimming in the damn thing.

But it was nice by the river at night. You could look over and see the Triborough, and downtown you could see the lights of the ferry going to Welfare Island, and if you looked hard you could see the U.N. all lit up like the streets are when it's *La Madonna di Carmena*. And out past the Triborough, you could get a glimpse maybe once in a while of North Brother Island where they got the hospital for teen-age junkies. It was kind of a sad idea, them kids out there sweating it out. I ain't a teen-ager. I'm twenty already, but I still got a feeling for kids like that who are all screwed up. It was Jobbo who suggested the Drive because he figured the lover-boys would park their cars there and then take the chicks onto the benches where they could watch the river. You couldn't park right on the Drive itself, naturally, but you could park in the side streets west of the Drive, and that's what Jobbo was counting on.

We worked it the way Jobbo suggested. We drifted along close to the river, walking past the benches and the rail. When we spotted a couple necking, we walked right past them a block or so, and then doubled back on the other side of the Drive. Then we checked the cars in the side street.

The first street we tried, we found three cars with the windows rolled down. The first two cars had nothing on the seats, and

I was too chicken to sit around and try the glove compartments. The third car had a magazine and a flashlight on the back seat. Jobbo stuck his hand in through the window, unlocked the door, and then grabbed the flashlight, leaving the magazine where it was.

'Here,' he said, handing me the flash. 'I'm gonna try the glove compartment.'

He rolled over onto the front seat and thumbed open the glove compartment and stuck his hands into it. I watched him for a second and then looked off down the street nervously. There wasn't a soul in sight, so I began to feel a little better.

'Anything in there?' I asked.

'Yeah,' he said.

'What?'

'I can't tell. Give me the flash.'

'We'll check it later. Come on, grab it and let's go.'

'Okay.'

He came out of the car and closed the front door behind him. We walked up to the Drive like a couple of old buddies out for a little stroll, and we stopped at the first empty bench we saw. Jobbo dug into his pocket and showed me what he'd swiped from the car.

'A compact,' I said.

'Yeah, I wonder if those are real rubies.'

'Rubies, my ass,' I said. 'You can pick up the same thing in the five-and-ten.'

'Well, the night is young,' Jobbo said.

'I think I had enough.'

'Whattya mean?'

'Just what I said. You think I'm gonna risk a hassle with the Law over this crap? What'll the flash bring you? A dime? And that compact? Your connection'll throw you out, you bring him this kind of crap.'

'Hell, you only just started,' Jobbo said. 'Three cars in the first block we tried. Don't get chicken now.'

'I ain't chicken. I just don't want to monkey with this petty horse manure, that's all.'

'Come on, let's give it another try.'

12

'Well, okay,' I said, 'but only one more block. We don't strike then, I'm going home.'

'We'll strike,' Jobbo said. 'Come on.'

We didn't look for nobody necking this time. We just walked up to the next block and started right away looking for open cars. We spotted one close to the corner, but it was too near the lamppost, so we let it pass. The sixth car up from the corner had the back window rolled down halfway.

'Here's another one,' Jobbo said.

I put the swiped flash up to the window and threw the beam onto the back seat. 'A coat,' I said, really surprised to see it.

'There, what'd I tell you!' Jobbo said triumphantly. 'Duck the light.'

I doused the flash, and Jobbo stuck his hand in and opened the door. He threw me the coat and then climbed over the front seat, breathing hard, trying the glove compartment. The coat wasn't an expensive one, I could see. Just a light wool job, without even a silk lining. The owner probably used it to spread under the car when he got a flat.

'Son of a bitch!' Jobbo said from the front seat.

'What is it?'

'A gun,' he said.

'Whattya mean?'

'A gun, a gun,' Jobbo said excitedly. 'Don't you know what the hell a gun is?'

'Put it back,' I said quickly. 'Come on, Jobbo, put it back. Let's cut out.'

'Don't you know what a gun'll bring us?' he whispered.

'Put it back,' I said. 'Suppose somebody got cooled with the damn thing?'

I looked down the street again. The lampposts cast circles of light on the corners and in the middle of the block. Up near First Avenue, I could see the traffic whizzing by. I heard Jobbo sniffing, and I turned back to the car.

'What are you doing? Come on, let's –'

'I'm smelling the barrel,' Jobbo said. 'Hell, this gun ain't been fired in years. The guy probably keeps it in the glove compartment for protection.'

'For Christ's sake, Jobbo, put it back, will you?' I was beginning to sweat a little. I didn't like the idea of the gun, and
I didn't want to mess with it. That was as stupid as swimming
in a polluted river. Besides, Jobbo was taking a hell of a lot
of time in the heap. 'You coming?' I whispered.

'I'm coming,' he said. I saw him slide across the front seat to
behind the wheel. Then he opened the door and stepped onto the
sidewalk. 'Let's go,' he said.

We walked up toward the Drive again. I kept looking back
over my shoulders.

'You know what this gun here'll bring us?' Jobbo said.

'You *took* the friggin' thing?' I shouted.

'Sure, I took it. Now quiet down,' he said. 'Man, we can get
a sawbuck each out of this.'

'Is it loaded?' I asked, wetting my lips. I saw Jobbo begin to
fiddle with it, and I said, 'Goddamnit, don't play with it! You
want it to go off in your face?'

'How can I tell if it's loaded unless I open it up?'

'Well, not here. Not while we're walking. Jesus, why'd you
have to take it, anyway? I don't like the idea of a gun.'

'This is a good gun,' Jobbo said seriously.

I didn't answer him. We kept walking up toward the Drive,
and then we crossed the Drive and headed downtown. I could
hear the noise of the tugs on the river and, under that, like a
drummer using brushes on a snare, the sound of the river
rushing against the wooden pilings. We kept walking until we
found a dark bench, and then we sat down. I had the coat
slung over one arm, and I was holding the flashlight in my left
hand.

Jobbo took the gun in his hands and brought it to where I
could get a good look at it.

'It's a .45,' he said.

'How can you tell?'

'Don't you know a .45 when you see one?' He seemed pretty
disgusted with me, but how the hell was I supposed to know
what a .45 looked like? 'Let's see if it's loaded,' he said.

'You sure you know what you're doing?'

'Don't worry about me, man,' Jobbo said. He poked around

14

the gun a little, and then a piece in the handle slid out like a drawer. 'Wow!' Jobbo said.

'What's the matter?'

'Nothing. It's got a full magazine, that's all.'

'Throw it in the river, will you?' I said. 'Do me a favor, Jobbo.'

'Like hell I will!' He slammed the little drawer back into the butt of the gun, and then he hefted the gun on his palm. 'Man,' he said, '*that* is a weapon!'

'Jobbo – '

'You see this little thing here? On the left-hand side of the piece? Right here, up near my thumb?'

'Yeah.' I leaned over, interested now. This was the first time I'd seen a real gun up close.

'That's your safety,' Jobbo said. 'You snap that on, and you can't fire the piece.'

'Is it on now?'

'Sure.' Jobbo snapped the little lever. 'There, now it's off. Now we can shoot the hell out of anybody.'

I got nervous again. 'Jobbo, throw it in the river.'

'Don't be a nut, Frankie,' he said. 'My connection'll blow his wig when he sees this. This is like money in the bank.' He paused, nodding. 'Yessir, money in the bank. Let's take a look at the coat we got.'

'I don't think it's any good,' I said.

'Well, let's have a look at it.'

I handed him the coat, and I watched while he turned it inside out, looking for a label. 'Cheap coat,' he said, 'but it might bring a deuce, who knows?'

'A deuce? For that?'

'Sure. Clean it up a little, you be surprised how much my connection'll get for this.' He found the label and tried to read it, but the bench was too dark. 'Hand me that flash, will you?'

I started to give him the flashlight, but he had the coat in one hand and the .45 in the other.

'Here,' he said. 'You hold the gun.'

'Jobbo, I don't like – '

'Come on, it won't bite you.'

I took the .45, and I felt my hand beginning to sweat against the grip. Jobbo flicked on the flash and was looking at the label inside the coat when I heard the sound of the engine. I turned my head. A Snow White was pulling up to the curb. My heart rushed up into my skull. For a second, I couldn't say anything, and then all I could do was say one word, 'Jobbo!'

'Whuh?'

He turned on the bench, looking over to the curb where the squad car had parked.

'The cops,' he said.

'Jobbo, what – ?'

He was up already. He moved faster than I thought a fat guy could move. He dropped the coat and the flash and he started sprinting uptown on the Drive.

'Come on!' he yelled, and it took me another second to get off the bench and start after him. I still had the .45 in my hand.

'Hold up there!' one of the cops yelled.

'Frig you, copper!' Jobbo yelled back, running ahead of me, his shoes clattering noisily on the asphalt.

'Stop or we'll shoot!' the cop yelled.

'Jobbo, they're gonna – '

The first shot sounded godawful loud on the quiet air. I heard it, and I automatically began running faster. I remembered something about the first shot always being over your head. I remembered, too, that they shot for your legs after that. That was the way Pasco got shot in the leg. So I kept running faster, waiting for the second shot, expecting it to knock my pins from under me. The next two shots came one after the other, *bohm*, *bohm!* like two fast beats on a bass drum. I didn't hear the fourth shot but I felt the bullet rip into my leg and I thought, *Oh, Jesus, I'm hit!* and then I was pitching forward, like as if someone had stuck out his foot and tripped me by surprise.

'I got him!' the cop yelled, as if he was surprised too, as if I was the first guy he'd ever shot in his life. I rolled over on the asphalt, feeling the pain burning my calf where the bullet had caught me. Jobbo stopped running, doubling back for me, you've got to give that to him, he didn't just leave me laying there. The cop who'd shot me came running from the other side, the gun still in his hand.

Behind me, I heard Jobbo shout, 'Open up on him, Frankie!' and I didn't know what he meant at first, and then I remembered I was holding the .45 in my hand. The cop was closer now, a big, red-faced guy waving his gun like a flag. A second cop had come out of the cruiser and was running toward us now, too. Maybe I wouldn't have shot, maybe I would have just tried to bluff it through, but Jobbo was right next to me now, sweating like a pig, his hands in my armpits, trying to get me up off the street.

'The gun!' he said. 'For Christ's sake, use the gun!'

I brought the gun up, and my hand was trembling like a bitch in heat, and I heard the first cop yell, 'He's heeled, George!' and then I pulled the trigger. It was just like with a toy gun, the same way – you pull it, and it goes off. Except the gun bucked in my hand, and a flash of yellow-orange spit out of the muzzle and the explosion was a big *BOHHMMMM!* that echoed on the night. The first cop suddenly fell forward on his face, and Jobbo yelled, 'You got him!' and then, for no good reason, I pulled the trigger again.

I kept firing at the first cop, watching his body give a sort of a little leap every time I hit him. I fired three times, and then I heard more shots, not as deep as the ones the .45 was making, and I realized the second cop was in the act now, shooting at me.

He was laying flat on the street, with his gun hand resting on a crooked elbow, and he took careful aim as Jobbo said, 'You got three left, Frankie. Make them good.'

I was up on one knee now with Jobbo behind me, bracing me. I guess it was comical the way we looked, him propping me up, and me holding that big damn gun in both hands and looking down the barrel and lining up the cop's body in the sight. He fired and missed, and I heard the slug sing by, and then I squeezed the trigger, and the .45 bucked in my hand again, once, twice, and the cop threw himself forward with a small scream, his gun jumping out of his hand and making a funny *thwunk* sound when it hit the ground. He lay very still then.

'Come on,' Jobbo said. He was excited now, and sweating, and I could smell the stink of him, but I only kept looking at the two cops sprawled unmoving on the street, the squad car parked about fifteen feet behind them. 'Come on, come on,' Jobbo kept saying, and then he had my arm over his shoulders, and he half-carried me, half-dragged me up to Pleasant Avenue. I stuck the gun back in my pocket. My leg hurt like hell. On First Avenue, I said, 'Where we going, Jobbo?'

'My connection,' he answered.

2

'He won't like it,' I said. 'Bringing me there. Jobbo, my leg's all shot up. I'm bleeding. I – '

'He'll take care of you, don't worry.'

I was beginning to get real scared. I was beginning to realize I'd shot and probably killed two cops, and I know how bulls felt about members of their club getting hurt. My leg was beginning to feel like it was on fire, little flames licking and burning and then dying and then licking again. I didn't want to look down at it because I knew it was all bloody, and looking at it might make me sick.

'Jobbo,' I said. 'Those two cops. They – '

'You did fine,' Jobbo answered. 'You did real fine. Now don't worry about a thing, you hear? My connection'll take care of it.'

I nodded, but I still wasn't convinced, and I still couldn't stop worrying. Jobbo kept walking with my arm over his shoulder. It was pretty late and there weren't many people in the streets. We got a few looks but you could see they thought I was a drunk being carried by a pal. One guy noticed my leg and shook his head, but he didn't figure I'd got shot, he just thought I'd been in some kind of an accident.

We went up 119th, past a candy store between Second and Third, and then Jobbo started dragging me up the stoop of one of the buildings. It was just one of the regular buildings, with the garbage cans out front near the curb, and the stoop with iron railings, one of these big gray jobs that are in all the streets of Harlem. I was a little surprised because I figured Jobbo's connection was a big man, and here he lived in a dump just like my own on 117th.

'He lives *here?*' I asked.

'Sure,' Jobbo answered. 'Come on.'

I looked over my shoulder, across the street to the schoolyard where some young boys and girls were hanging around. They were laughing and clowning, you know, the way kids do when they get together. They weren't even looking in our direction. Jobbo helped me inside and then past the mailboxes. There was the smell of piss in the hallway. We had trouble trying to get up the steps, but Jobbo helped me all the way. We kept climbing, and then we stopped on the third-floor landing. Jobbo looked back down the steps, but there was nobody behind us. Then he helped me hobble to a door at the end of the hall.

'Now just let me do the talking,' he said.

'All right.' I think I was ready to pass out by then. He could have talked all night if he wanted to. All I wanted to do was lay down some place and forget about the pain in my leg. He knocked on the door and, considering it was almost one in the morning, I wasn't surprised we didn't get an answer right off.

'Look, Jobbo,' I said weakly, 'maybe we better forget this. The guy's probably sleeping. You wake him up, he'll – '

'It's okay,' Jobbo said. He knocked again, harder this time. A voice from somewhere inside the apartment said, 'Who is it?' The voice was a big one, the kind you expect to come from a guy with a hairy chest.

'It's me. Jobbo.'

I heard a grumbling inside and then the voice said, 'Just a minute.' The voice sounded angry as hell.

'Jobbo,' I said, 'he's sore. We're getting him out of bed. Can't you see – ?'

'Now just shut up and let me do the talking,' Jobbo said.

I heard footsteps inside the apartment, and then a police lock was moved back from the door, the heavy steel bar clattering to the floor. Then the door opened a crack, held by a thick night chain. It was dark in the hallway, and I could hardly see the face that showed in the crack.

'What is it?' the voice said. 'You know what time it is, for Christ's sake?'

'Andy, we need your help. We – '

'Who's that with you?' Andy asked.

'A friend of mine,' Jobbo said. 'Can you let us in?'

Andy peered through the crack for what seemed like a long time. Then he said, 'All right, goddamnit!' and he took off the night chain and held the door open just wide enough for us to squeeze through.

'You better get some newspapers,' Jobbo said. 'His leg's bleeding pretty bad.'

'Okay,' Andy said, and he started walking toward the kitchen and then did one of those double takes you see all the time in the movies. He snapped his head around, and his mouth fell open, and then he closed his mouth, and then he opened it and said, 'Bleeding! What the hell – '

'Shhh,' Jobbo warned.

'What the hell you mean, *bleeding?*' Andy said, his voice lower. He was as big as he'd first sounded, and he was in his shorts and undershirt, with heavy hairy legs sticking out of the bottom of the shorts. He still hadn't turned on any of the lights, but the shade in the living room was up, and I could see him from the light that came through the window.

From deeper in the apartment, I heard a woman call, 'Who is it, Andy?'

Andy looked at us sourly and then shouted, 'Some friends. Go back to sleep.'

'What friends?' the woman called, but Andy didn't answer her this time. He looked at me, and then he looked at my leg, and then he got the most disgusted look I've ever seen on anybody's face. 'I'll get some newspapers,' he said. 'Did the Law follow you?'

'No,' Jobbo said.

Andy nodded briefly and went into the kitchen, snapping on a light. I heard him fooling around in one of the drawers, and when he came back he had a bunch of old newspapers in his hand.

'Sit down,' he said gruffly. He turned on a table lamp, and I hobbled over to the sofa, ready to sit. 'Not there, for Christ's sake! My wife'll have a fit. Over there.'

He pointed to the beat-up easy chair near the window, and I limped to it and sat down. It felt good to be sitting again. He spread the newspapers under me, and I watched the blood running down my leg, turning the paper soggy and red, and it occurred to me that somebody better stop all that blood before my life ran out of that hole.

'All right, what's the story?' Andy asked Jobbo.

'We had a run-in with the cops,' Jobbo said.

'I figured. Did they get a good look at you?'

'Sure,' Jobbo said, smiling. 'But that ain't gonna do them any good.'

'What do you mean?'

'Frankie fixed them,' he said, still smiling.

'How so? How'd he fix them?'

'They're both dead,' Jobbo said. 'We swiped this .45, you see? And Frankie was holding the gun when – '

'Are you sure they're dead?'

'Huh?'

'Are you sure they're dead? Did you check?'

'Well . . . no. We ran. I mean . . . well, what the hell, Andy! We couldn't stick around and do an autopsy!'

'Then they maybe ain't dead, is that what you're saying?'

'They're dead,' I said.

'How do you know?' Andy asked, turning to me.

'I know. I can feel it. They're dead.'

He looked at me peculiarly for a minute. Then he just nodded his head. 'Where's the gun?'

'I got it,' I told him.

'Give it to me.'

I took the gun out of my pocket and handed it to him. I was beginning to feel very weak. Or maybe just tired. I don't know. But I felt as if I never wanted to get up out of that chair. Andy sniffed the barrel, and I wondered was he going to sit down and take the gun apart maybe while I bled to death? 'We'll have to get rid of this,' he said. Then he looked at my leg, at last, and yelled, 'Celia! Come here, Celia!'

'What is it, Andy?' the woman called.

'Never mind what it is! Come here when I tell you!'

'It's sure bleeding, ain't it?' Jobbo said. 'Man, it's – '

'Where you live, kid?' Andy cut in.

'A Hun' Seventeenth.'

22

'With your folks?'

'Only my mother. My old man is dead.'

'You got a record? You ever been booked?'

'Never.'

'You telling me the truth?'

'I never been in trouble with the Law,' I said.

'He's clean,' Jobbo said. 'I know him for a long time, Andy.'

Andy nodded and turned to me again. 'What about the rest of your family? Any arrests?'

'Listen – '

'Tell him what he wants to know, Frankie,' Jobbo said.

'I got an uncle at Riker's, that's all.'

'What for?'

'Holding,' I said.

'Just holding? Or pushing?'

'Pushing.'

'The big stuff?'

'Cocaine, I think. How the hell should I know? I hardly ever saw the guy. He's my old man's brother.'

'*Celia!*' Andy exploded. '*When the hell –* '

'I'm coming, keep your shirt on,' the woman answered, and then I heard her footsteps in the other room. From her voice, I expected a kind of a dog, if you know what I mean. I guess that's because we woke her up in the middle of the night and people always sound like hell when you drag them out of bed. She wasn't half-bad, though. She came through the door, and she was a tall blonde with a silk wrapper thrown over her night-gown, and her hair sort of spilled over one eye, still all messed up from sleeping. She didn't have on any lipstick or make-up, so I knew the long lashes were her own, and I knew she wasn't using anything to make her green eyes look that big.

She stopped near the television set, and then she put her hands on her hips and looked at Jobbo and then at me, and her eyes dropped to the newspapers and my leg right away.

'What's this?' she said. 'The Harlem Hospital clinic?'

'Never mind the wisecracks,' Andy said. 'Get some bandages. And hurry up before he bleeds to death.'

'He won't bleed to death,' she said.

She walked across the room. Jobbo wet his lips, but Andy didn't notice him because he was looking over the gun again.

'Where'd you say you got this?' he asked.

'From a parked car,' Jobbo said. Celia was already in the kitchen, and I heard her open the bathroom door, and then the door to the medicine chest.

'That's good,' Andy said. 'Even if Ballistics gets anything on the slugs, they won't be able to trace the gun to you. That's very good.'

'What're we gonna do, Andy?' Jobbo asked.

'Well, if the cops are really dead, and what with the gun not even belonging to you, this should be a cinch. Can you stay away from home for a while, kid?'

'How do you mean?'

'If we get you out of the city, can you square it with your old lady?'

'Sure. I been away before,' I paused. 'She don't know whether I'm dead or alive, anyway.'

I didn't bother telling him that she was most of the time drunk, or that she spent the welfare allowance on booze. There was no sense trying to explain it. She'd been that way ever since my old man died, first drinking up all the damn insurance money and then drinking up every cent she could lay her hands on. I didn't even like to think about it. I could remember my mother when she dressed nice and smelled nice, and when she made a kid feel proud he had a good-looking mother. Now, at forty-two, she looked like just what she was: an old drunk.

'Good,' Andy said. 'If the cops are dead, they sure can't tell anyone you've been wounded.' He shook his head immediately. 'No, you probably left blood. It'll be safer all around if we get you out of the city. Hey, Celia, you getting those bandages?'

I heard her footsteps again, and then she was back in the room. I watched her carefully this time. She saw me watching, but her face didn't show any sign of it. She stopped right in front of me and she looked at my leg again and then she said, 'You better come in the bedroom.'

'Good idea,' Andy said. 'I want to talk to Jobbo alone, anyway.'

Jobbo helped me into the bedroom, and Celia followed us. I sat down on the edge of the bed. Jobbo looked at my leg, worried now.

'Come here, Jobbo,' Andy said. 'Few things I want to ask you. Celia'll take care of him.'

Jobbo went back into the living room and sat next to Andy. 'What about this kid?' Andy said. 'What's his name, and how long – ' He cut himself short and looked over his shoulder. 'Close that door, Celia,' he said.

Celia walked to the door and closed it tightly and the room was suddenly completely dark. I could hear her breathing in the room, and then her footsteps coming toward me in the darkness. I held my breath. A lamp clicked on next to the bed. Celia smiled at me.

'Who shot you?'

'A cop.'

'Oh, that's nice,' she said sarcastically. 'That's just dandy. You sure you weren't followed here?'

'I killed him and his partner,' I said. I was getting used to saying it. The idea didn't scare me so much any more.

She raised her eyebrows and looked at me appreciatively, and then she stared down at my soggy pants leg.

'You'd better take off your pants.'

'Couldn't we just roll – ?'

'Take them off.'

I swung my legs up onto the bed and undid my belt. I lifted my backside and shoved the pants down over my thighs. I was a little embarrassed, to tell the truth. Besides her being a woman, I was also wearing cheap cotton undershorts which I'd bought in Woolworth's. I used to have a job before the summer, you see, working in a dry-goods store. But it was slow during the summer, and the owner had to lay me off, not that I blamed him – what the hell, he wasn't in business for his health. But with the old lady drinking up any money the city gave us, there wasn't much left for fancy clothes. So my undershorts were cheap, and I was embarrassed by them.

Celia helped me pull the pants off, easing them over my legs.

'We may need a doctor on this,' she said. 'Is the bullet still in there?'

'How should I know?'

'Can't you feel it?'

'I can't feel nothing below the knee.'

She came over to the bed and sat down. She bent over and the silk wrapper fell loose in the front, and the gown under the wrapper was nothing but cheesecloth practically. I could see her almost as if she was bare, and she knew I could see her but she didn't do nothing to pull the wrapper closed. She kept leaning over, looking at my leg, and then she said, 'This looks pretty bad. I'm gonna tell Andy to get a doctor.'

She lifted her head, catching my eyes on the front of her gown. She stared at me for a second, and I lowered my eyes, ashamed because she'd caught me looking. She raised her eyebrows just a tiny bit, as if she was surprised – but I knew she wasn't – and then she smiled a very little and slid off the bed, walking to the door, swinging her hips more than she had before. She opened the door just a crack, and I heard Andy saying, ' . . . and he's never been in a jam before, is that right? You can vouch for that?'

Jobbo didn't get a chance to answer. Celia interrupted him with, 'You better call Murray on this, Andy. I can clean the leg, but that's all. It's pretty bad.'

'All right, clean it,' Andy said. 'I'll call Murray when I get done here. Close the door.'

She shrugged and closed the door, and then she walked back to the bed, looking down at me, her hands on her hips, a smile on her mouth. 'I'll get some alcohol,' she said. She crossed the room to the door again, stopped before opening it, and said, 'Don't go away, boy.' Then she went out.

I lay back on the bed, looking the joint over. It was really nothing special, the usual railroad flat you find all over East Harlem, the chipped plaster, the peeling paint, the big ugly radiator. The room was furnished with a bargain set you could pick up in any of the cheap furniture stores. A big picture of Jesus suffering on the cross was over the bed, and a candle burned in a light red glass thing on the dresser, probably for somebody who was dead. There was a smell in the room – I got a very sensitive nose, you probably gathered by now – and I recognized it was perfume. But the perfume didn't hide the fact that the apartment was a dump. Whatever Andy was, he wasn't no wheel, that was for sure. Unless this was all a front, and that didn't seem hardly possible. He certainly seemed to know the right people to contact, though, and I wasn't gonna look no gift horse in the mouth. Without his help ...

The door opened again, and Celia came in. Outside in the living room, I could see Andy dialing the phone. The phone was covered with one of these cheap plastic things that's supposed to make it look like an expensive colored telephone, only it don't. It makes it look like a black telephone covered with a cheap plastic thing. Celia closed the door and walked over to the bed. She doused a rag with alcohol and then she sat down and went to work on my leg.

I'm not a baby. I mean, I had things happen to me before, things that hurt. Like once I busted my arm playing football in the street. Not really football. We used to roll up a newspaper and tie it with a piece of cord, or sometimes a rubber band, and this made a long cylinder which we used for a ball. The name of the game, actually, was Touchball, I guess. Anyway, I busted my arm because this kid named Tommy threw a pass, and I was running for it, looking back at the ball, and I ran right into a parked car and I busted my arm. That really hurt. I mean, my leg hurt right then too, but the arm that time had really hurt like á bastard. I'm not trying to be a hero or any-thing. I'm only trying to say that though the alcohol stung when she poured it on the wound, it wasn't real pain like the time I busted my arm. So I didn't expect her to mention anything about it, but she wiped the wound and made it nice and clean, and then she looked at me and said, 'You're a brave kid,' and then she kissed me.

It was a real quick kiss, her mouth was there one minute and the next minute it was gone. It surprised the hell out of me because even though she was walking around half-naked, I certainly didn't expect to be kissed, even a quick kiss like that.

She stood up and smiled at me and I didn't know what to say and maybe it's better I didn't say nothing because right then the door opened and Andy walked in with Jobbo behind him.

'How's it going?' Andy asked, smiling. I guess he was happy about the way his phone call turned out. I kept thinking how he wouldn't have been so happy if he'd walked into the room about two minutes earlier.

'Fine,' Celia said. She turned to me. 'We're doing fine, aren't we, boy?'

'Yeah,' I said.

'Murray'll be over in a few minutes,' Andy said, 'and I got a car coming in about a half-hour. You ever been to Jersey, kid?'

'A few times,' I said.

'We got a motel in Jersey. We can put you up there until the leg's all right.'

'*You* got a motel in Jersey?' I asked.

'Me?' Andy chuckled. 'No, not me, kid.' He paused. 'Murray'll look over your leg when he gets here. He used to be a very high-priced doctor, kid.'

They stood around the bed, with Celia sitting at the foot now. With Andy in the room, she didn't even look at me. I began to think maybe she hadn't kissed me after all. Maybe I was just delirious or something.

'Why are you doing all this for me?' I asked.

'Why not?' Andy said.

'Sure, it's nice of you. But why?'

'You sound pretty handy with a gun.'

'Are you kidding?' I said.

'You killed two cops, didn't you? Jobbo told me how cool you were.'

'That was the first time I ever had a gun in my hand,' I said. 'I don't know a gun from a – '

'Imagine when you've had a little practice, kid,' Andy said.

'Practice? What do you – ?'

We heard a knock on the door. Andy said, 'There's Murray now.' He walked out of the bedroom, and Jobbo followed behind him.

'What did he mean?' I asked Celia. 'About practice?'

'They've probably got room for somebody who can use a gun, that's all,' Celia said.

'But I can't – '

'Go along with it, boy,' she said. 'It'll be interesting.' She was sitting at the foot of the bed. She lifted one hand and put it on my ankle, and her fingers tightened there. 'You'll get lots of practice, boy,' she said, and her eyes held mine. She nodded her head, unsmilingly, and then pulled her hand back when she heard footsteps coming toward the bedroom.

'Murray, meet Frankie,' Andy said, coming into the room with a hawk-faced, serious-looking guy. Murray nodded, glancing briefly at my leg.

'Why do they always get shot in the middle of the night?' he said sourly. Andy laughed, and Celia laughed too, a high laugh the crack didn't warrant. I looked at her. Her face was flushed, and her eyes were sparkling. Murray took off his jacket and then rolled up his sleeves. His arms were skinny and covered with thick black hair, but his hands looked strong. He blinked behind his glasses and then walked to the bed.

'All right,' he said, 'let's have a look at it,' and then in the same breath, without even looking at her, 'Hello, Celia.'

'Fix him up good, Murray,' Andy said. 'He's a good boy.'

3

They took me to a town named Spotswood, and then out past the town to a small motel off the main highway. The motel had about a dozen cabins and another cabin that served as the office. A guy named Dirk was in charge of the operation, but he didn't own the place, either, and after I was there a while he told me he was on salary.

It didn't take me long to figure out what the motel was. I ain't the smartest guy in the world, that's a cinch, but I'm pretty quick on the uptake. The trade at the motel was usually at night, and I never saw any young kids in the crowd. The cars would pull up to the cabins around eight thirty or so, and then leave around midnight. Whatever the place was, you could bet it hadn't been recommended by the AAA. Nobody came to my cabin, and nobody went to Cabin Three, either. I found out from Dirk that Three was 'occupied,' but he wouldn't tell me nothing about who was in it.

In all the time I was there, not a single cop came to visit the place. Murray came to see me every day. He told me I was lucky that cops carry .38's and not .45's because a .45 can leave a very nasty hole which takes a long time to heal. He said I would have been luckier still if cops carried .22's, which they don't, because a .22 makes a very tiny hole which you got to search for to find, and which heals pretty quick. As it was, he said I'd be on my back for about three weeks, and that the wound would be scabbed over by that time, and eventually I'd have a little scar on my leg. He had to change the dressing on the wound every day because he said there was a lot of drainage. He also didn't want me to get gangrene or anything and so he put me on some pills which he said was a 'broad spectrum antibiotic.' I guess he meant penicillin. He was a very educated man, Murray, and he never used a simple word where a complicated word would do. For example, he said I had 'remarkable recuperative powers,' when all he meant was I healed pretty quick.

He didn't tell me much about himself, but what he told me was enough. Like I said, I'm pretty fast on the uptake. He would drop little things from time to time, and the little things didn't mean nothing until you put them all together and then they spelled out how come a guy like Murray was fixing up a guy who'd got in trouble with the cops. I found out, for example, that he went to med school at Cornell and was among the top ten in his class. He didn't tell me that directly, it just sort of came out in conversation, a sort of sarcastic remark he was making about himself. I also found out that he used to practice medicine in a town called New Canaan, which is in Connecticut someplace and which is mostly full of Madison Avenue advertising guys.

At first I figured maybe Murray had lost his license because he did an abortion or something. That seemed pretty corny, and it's always what you see in the movies, the noted brain surgeon who could have discovered the cancer cure, for Christ's sake, if he hadn't goofed just that once and helped out his maiden aunt who got knocked up by the local minister. Well, Murray lost his license not because he was a good guy but because he was a rat, which shows what the movie people know. Living in this town of New Canaan, Murray began to suspect that some guy was playing around with his wife. He kept trying to figure out a way to put the blocks to the guy, but his chance didn't come until one night the guy got involved in an automobile accident and Murray was called in by the troopers to take the usual ten c.c.'s of blood for the blood-alcohol test to find out whether the guy was crocked or not.

Well, the guy wasn't crocked. He hadn't even been drinking at all. But Murray took his sponge and wiped it on the guy's arm just before he took the blood sample. The sponge was sopping with alcohol. Murray stuck his needle through the alcohol smear and into the guy's arm, taking enough alcohol – two-tenths of a milligram would have been enough, Murray said

– in with the blood to contaminate the test. The guy was accused of drunken driving. Murray thought he'd done a great job. Except that the trooper who'd brought the guy to Murray happened to see him wipe the guy's arm with the alcohol-soaked sponge. So the trooper went to bat for the guy and Murray was found guilty of 'fraud or deceit in the practice of medicine,' and that was enough to cause the yanking of his license.

I gather he knocked around a long time before he fell back again on the only thing he really knew: medicine. Only, of course, he couldn't legally practice any more, so he had to practice illegally, and that's how come he was the guy who dressed my leg that night and took care of it all the while I was in Spotswood. I was thankful, believe me. A legit medic would have had to report the gun wound. And there was no danger of that with Murray.

I did a lot of thinking up there in Spotswood.

There wasn't much else to do, you see. I wasn't allowed out of the cabin, not even to walk around the grounds. Dirk brought me my meals, and sometimes he stayed for a few games of checkers or a round of pinochle, but most of the time I was alone. I never liked reading, so I hardly touched any of the pocket books Dirk brought. I just laid on the bed mostly and looked up at the ceiling, remembering that night with the cops, and remembering too the kiss from Celia.

I'd killed those cops, all right. There was no doubt about that. The newspapers had carried the full story the next day, and then a follow-up story the day afterwards. During the next two weeks, I watched the story get smaller and smaller as the police leads fizzled out. The last time they ran it, it was buried in the middle of the newspaper, a small item over an almost full-page Macy's ad. I knew this wasn't the end of it. I mean, cops never let go of something. You're always reading about them picking up a guy on a drunk charge or something and they go to work on him, and it turns out he done the Brink's robbery years back. Like that. So I figured my best bet was to keep away from the cops from now on, otherwise I'd be like they say, up the creek. But I wasn't taking any credit away from Andy and the people he worked for. I was safe in Spotswood. My leg was healing. And the cops had put the case on ice for now. So I was grateful to Andy.

But the more I thought about his helping hand, the more I wondered about it. I liked being helped, sure, but I didn't like what I figured was expected in payment. Now don't misunderstand I'm a welsher or anything like that. I ain't. I've always paid the piper, and I was willing to give Andy and his higher-ups anything reasonable for helping me. It was on the 'reasonable' that we might have a little trouble, I figured. To make it short, I didn't like the idea of being considered a torpedo. What the hell, I'd shot those cops in self-defense, sort of. When the heat's on, you'll do anything to get yourself out of the soup. All right, the cops happened to hand in their chips, but that didn't make me a killer, not in the sense Andy was thinking of. I knew I should have told him that the night Jobbo took me to his pad, and I'd really tried to tell him, but then I figured it was best to keep quiet until the leg was better. But I wasn't going to run around killing anybody else, no matter what they thought.

Celia was something else again. Now I'm pretty hip to the sex bit. I've had it, you know, and a broad's a broad. But Celia was maybe thirty years old or around there, and there's something gets me excited about an older dame. I don't know what it is, except you think they've got a little more experience and know just what they want. Whatever, an old dame has always seemed more passionate to me, and I sure as hell didn't mistake that kiss she gave me. But there was still Andy to consider, and he wasn't exactly no shrimp, not with that chest and those arms, and not even mentioning his connection with the higher-ups. Celia was something, and I filed her away under Unfinished Business, but I didn't want a hassle with Andy over her, and I didn't want a hole in the head some night, either.

So I thought about all these things, waiting for the day I could leave Spotswood. I decided finally to play it cool and see which way the cards fell.

The leg healed in about three weeks, just like Murray said it would. He came in one Saturday, and there was the stink of booze on his breath, and he gave me an examination and said I could join the human race again in a few days. Those were his exact words. He didn't much like the human race, Murray. He always talked about humans as if they were only animals who just by luck discovered how to stand up and use their front paws. Anyway, he said he'd call Andy, and I guess he did because Andy showed up on Monday morning.

He was driving an old Chevy, not that I was expecting a Cadillac, but I still found it hard getting used to the idea of him living in a dump and driving a low-priced car. He pulled up in front of the office. I looked through the blinds, and when I recognized him I began to feel free already. He talked with Dirk for a few minutes, and then walked up the gravel to my cabin. He knocked on the door, and I asked, 'Who is it?' even though I knew it was him, just to show him I was being careful.

'It's Andy, kid,' he said. 'Open up.'

I opened the door for him and looked out at the Chevy. Celia was sitting in the back, and I felt my blood get a little quicker, and then I told myself to be careful, Andy was there.

'Walking around, huh, kid?' Andy said, smiling.

'I been walking for a long time,' I told him. 'Why don't you bring Celia in with you?'

'What for? You ready to leave?'

'Sure.'

'Then come on. No sense in hanging around.'

I went in the bathroom and got my toothbrush and razor, which I maybe used six or seven times all the while I was there. I don't have a very heavy beard. I got black hair and brown eyes, and lots of guys with that color combination have these thick, heavy five-o'clock-shadow things. But not me. I shave maybe every three days, and I look fine in between. The guys on the block used to rib me about the beard. They think to be a man you got to be hairy. Well, I ain't hairy, but that don't make me any less a man. I could knock down any guy on the block, that's the truth. I was fighting all the time when I was a kid. I figured out pretty early that the only way to get what you want is to show you want it. And nothing speaks louder than your hands. That's the truth. And there were plenty of five-o'clock-

34

shadow bums I knocked on their asses for just looking at me crooked. I just wanted you to know, in case you think a guy needs whiskers. He don't.

When I finished picking up the few things I had in the cabin, I went out to the car with Andy. I climbed in, and then turned on the seat to say hello to Celia, giving her a big smile. She didn't smile back. She had her legs crossed, and a gold ankle bracelet caught the sun and made it dance. She had good legs, and her dress was high enough to be showing a lot of them. I kept thinking how she was thirty years old or around there, and I began to get a little parched in the mouth.

'Hello, boy,' she said, and then she turned and fished a cigarette from her purse, lighting it without even looking at me. I swung around as Andy started the car.

'I'd like to say good-bye to Dirk and Murray,' I said.

'Murray already left,' Andy said, 'and the hell with Dirk. We've got a busy morning ahead of us.'

'Oh, yeah? Where we going?'

'You'll see. Learn not to ask too many questions, kid. It's better that way.'

'Sure, I was just – '

'How'd you like Spotswood?'

'I never even saw Spotswood. I never once got out of that cabin.'

'You got any complaints?' Andy said.

'No. No complaints.'

'Leave the boy alone,' Celia said. 'He's been cooped up for three weeks. Least he can do is – '

'Shut up, Celia,' Andy said. 'When I want your advice, I'll ask for it.'

'In three weeks,' Celia said, 'a person can get hungry.'

'How the hell would you know?' Andy asked.

'I've been cooped up all my life.'

'Now what the hell is that supposed to mean?'

'Nothing,' she said. 'Watch the road.'

Andy turned back toward the road, driving slowly and carefully. I guess when you're fooling around with the Law, you can't afford to get picked up on some crap thing like speeding or passing a red light. It's like a bank teller who's taking home a grand a week from the till. He always counts out pennies for the customers because he don't want some fishy-eyed accountant to find even the slightest little error, not when he's knocking himself out to cover that thousand-dollar deficit. I never yet rode with anybody who's ever brushed with the Law and seen him drive fast or careless. The best drivers in the world are crooks. That's a flat statement, take it or leave it. This don't mean if you're a good driver, you are also a crook. But if you're a crook, I guarantee you're a good driver. Andy was a careful good driver, even now when he was pissed off at his wife. He drove with this frown all over his face, and I guess he set the tone because nobody talked for a long time. Then, after a while, the frown went away, and he got a little jovial again.

'How was the service, kid?' he asked.

'Couldn't have been better.'

'Fine. You'll get our bill in the morning.' He laughed aloud, but nobody in the car laughed with him.

'I've been meaning to talk to you about that, Andy,' I said. 'About paying for – '

'Never mind. You'll get plenty opportunity to talk later on today.'

'Oh. Well sure, whatever you say.'

Now apparently Celia was steaming on the back seat all this time. She wasn't the kind of dame who takes guff from a man, and Andy had shut her up a while back, or anyway he thought he'd shut her up, but all he'd done was give her more coal for that fire she was building inside her.

'Let him talk!' she yelled. 'For Christ's sake, stop cutting him dead.'

Andy's eyebrows went up onto his forehead. He was opening his mouth when the next blast came from Celia.

'The kid's hungry for talk,' she said, 'can't you see that? He's been locked in with a clam like Murray and a moron like Dirk! It's a wonder he didn't go out of his mind!'

I turned on the seat. Her legs were still crossed, but her skirt was a little higher now, and she was jiggling the foot with the bracelet on it.

'Well, neither Murray or Dirk are what you'd call great conversationalists,' I said.

'I didn't think so,' Celia answered. 'You can talk to me, Frankie. If Andy doesn't feel like talking he can just keep watching the road.'

'Listen, talk,' Andy said. 'Talk your heads off, who cares? What the hell do I care if you talk or not?' He was getting angry all over again, but I could see he didn't figure any percentage in starting a ten-round bout with his wife. Whatever else she had, she also had a sharp tongue. I began to think maybe I should steer wide around this dame. That tongue could cut you to ribbons before you even knew you were being cut.

Celia looked in the rear-view mirror and her eyes met Andy's there. She sat where she was for a few minutes, and then she slid over on the seat, moving to the right of the car so that she was right behind me, where Andy couldn't see her in the mirror. She began jiggling her leg again. I looked at it, and then I looked at her face, and she smiled and winked at me. I dropped my hand carelessly over the back of the seat and my fingers brushed against her ankle.

'So let's talk, Frankie,' she said. 'Tell me what you did all the while you were up here.'

'There wasn't a hell of a lot *to* do,' I said. 'I just stayed in the cabin, that's all. And once in a while I played checkers with Dirk.'

'You should have asked him to get you a girl. Or aren't you interested in girls?'

'I'm interested, all right,' I said, and I caught her ankle with my hand, and I squeezed it, and she opened her mouth in a little sort of surprise, and then she kept moving her foot, twisting it under my hand.

'Is that so?' she said. 'Well, is that so?'

'Tell him all the nice things Jobbo's been saying about him,' Andy said. 'You feel like talking, tell him that.'

'Jobbo says you're a smart boy,' Celia said.

'He says that about everybody.'

'No, he don't,' Andy said. 'Jobbo's too stupid to say that about everybody. A smart boy tells *everybody* they're smart.

But Jobbo's stupid, so if he says somebody's smart, he means it. You follow?'

'Well . . . '

'No wells about it. We got room for a smart boy, Frankie.'

'That's what I wanted to talk to you about, Andy. I mean, I think you got the idea – '

'These people I'm taking you to meet,' Andy said, 'they know what to do with a smart boy. You working now, Frankie?'

'No,' I said.

'Then you wouldn't turn down something good that comes your way, would you?'

I turned halfway on the seat and looked at Celia. 'No, I wouldn't turn down nothing that looked good.'

'Besides, you kind of owe us a little something, don't you?'

'Well, you see, that's just it. This idea of – '

'Not that we'll hold that over your head, Frankie. You can just forget that, if you've got that on your mind. What we done for you was free and clear, no strings attached. You want to walk out now, that's perfectly all right, you understand?'

I got to admit I felt pretty relieved when he said that. I guess I almost sighed. 'Well, that's real nice of you, Andy. I appreciate it.'

'Not at all. That's the way we work.'

'Well, I sure appreciate it.'

'But you can go far with us, Frankie. Ain't that right, Celia?'

'You can go as far as you like, Frankie,' Celia said.

This was a weird thing, what was going on with her. I was holding her ankle, and she was twisting her foot, and I swear to God it was almost like being in bed together. That's crazy, I know. But just holding her ankle, just feeling her warm skin under the smooth nylon was better than kissing or hugging other girls. It's hard to explain, I know.

'Look at Andy,' Celia said with that sharp tongue of hers. 'Look at how far he's gone.'

'Yeah, don't get smart,' Andy said. 'I only been with the outfit a short time, Frankie, and I'm pulling down a cool two hundred a week. Is that chicken feed?'

'It sure ain't.'

'Sure, we live in a dump, but it wouldn't look good to move out all of a sudden. Besides, we need a good man on the scene, for emergencies, for things like what happened to you that night.'

'I see.'

'That's why we drive a Chevy,' Celia said sarcastically. 'We can afford a Lincoln, but we got to keep up appearances.'

'Don't listen to her,' Andy said. 'She's just an ungrateful bitch.'

'Thanks,' Celia said dryly.

'I like you, Frankie,' Andy said. 'And I'm slated for bigger stuff, believe me. I'm going to be a big man in this outfit, and if you stick around, who knows? There ain't no limit to what could happen to you. Provided you keep your nose clean and do what you're told in the beginning.'

'I'll keep my nose clean,' I said.

I kept my hand on Celia's ankle.

We drove over the George Washington Bridge, and then Andy kept driving downtown. He finally pulled up in front of a big building on Central Park West. I was sorry the ride was over. Even after what happened later, even after everything, I'll never forget that drive back from New Jersey when just touching Celia's leg made me weak. I'll never forget that as long as I live.

We all got out of the car and walked under the canopy to the front door, where a uniformed joker threw it open for us. We rang for the elevator in the lobby, and when it came, Andy stepped in first, the Indian Chief going ahead of the squaw. Celia frowned and walked in after him. I went in last. 'Twelve,' Andy said to the operator.

The car went up, and we got off. Andy led us down to a door at the end of the hall. He buzzed twice, and we waited until a small click told us the peephole was being looked through. It was one of those see-through-only-one-way jobs, so that we couldn't glimpse the eye looking out. We heard the click again, and a voice behind the door said, 'Oh, Andy,' and then I heard the chain going off the door, and then a lock being unlocked, and then another lock, and then I figured for Christ's sake we must be entering Fort Knox.

The door opened wide on a guy almost as fat as Jobbo. This guy was well-dressed, though, and I'd have bet my life he didn't stink the way Jobbo did. And if he did, it was probably from expensive cologne. His lapels were hand-stitched, and he was wearing a white-on-white shirt, and a silk tie with just a tiny small white horse's head design in one spot down below the knot. He wore a gold tie clasp high up on his tie, a little too high for my taste, but you could see it was real gold and not any cheap crap. I hate imitations. I always hated them, even when I was a kid. For me, it's got to be the genuine article, or nothing. So I could appreciate the tie clasp this guy was wearing, and the tailor-made suit, and the expensive shirt. I go for good things.

'Come on in, Andy,' the guy said. 'Ah, you brang the missus. Hello, Celia.' We stepped onto a thick rug, and the guy who'd opened the door for us took Celia into his arms and gave her a kiss on the cheek, the way my greaseball uncles and aunts used to do to my old man when he was still alive. 'Come in, kid,' he said to me, and then he closed the door. As Celia passed him, he dropped the uncle routine and patted her on the behind. It got me sore, his doing that, but I didn't say anything. I could see a bulge under the left hand side of his jacket, right where his monogrammed pocket handkerchief was, and I knew that bulge wasn't made by no muscle.

'Mr Carfon is waiting for you, Andy,' he said.

'Good. He knows I was bringing the kid, don't he?'

'Oh, sure.'

'How've things been going, Milt?'

'So-so,' he answered, smiling. 'I understand this is a good boy.' Andy nodded. Milt kept looking at me. 'He's too handsome, Andy,' he said, smiling. 'You better lock Celia in a closet.' He began laughing, and Andy laughed with him, and even Celia joined in until I began to feel a little stupid, the only one standing there and not laughing.

'So come on in,' Milt said when he was finished laughing. 'Turk's here already.'

'Oh, good,' Andy said. 'You think Mr Carfon'll mind? Me bringing Celia along?'

'Hell, no,' Milt said. 'Brighten up the joint a little, hah, Cele?'

'I'm just a little ray of sunshine,' Celia said, and Milt laughed again.

The rug was like walking on grass, well maybe not that thick, but plenty thick, plusher than any rug I'd ever walked on. The furniture was all this low, clean, modern stuff, with a lot of marble and wrought iron and highly polished woods around the room. A grand piano was at one end of the room, and behind that were windows all across the wall, so that the place was full of sunshine. Milt led us through the room and then stopped outside a paneled door at the end, and knocked twice, and soft.

'Yes?' a voice asked. It was a gentle voice, and from just the way that word 'Yes?' came through the door, I could tell the voice belonged to the one they called 'Mister.'

'Andy's here, Mr Carfon,' Milt said.

'Show him in, please,' Mr Carfon said.

Milt winked and opened the door. Andy stepped in first again, ignoring Celia. I was beginning to total Andy as a kind of a meathead. Every time he goofed in the little courtesies, Celia did a slow burn which he didn't seem to notice. This don't exactly promote marital harmony, so you'd imagine the guy would wise up and start pleasing the lady. Instead, he barged right into the room ahead of her. Milt gave Celia a sympathetic smile – I still hadn't forgot that friendly pat he gave her – and then let her and me go by him into the room. Then he closed the door after us and stayed outside.

The room was a big one, with the same thick rug on the floor. I was willing to bet that rug spread through the whole damn apartment, even the bathrooms. There were a few sofas in the room, off-the-floor modern stuff, and a bar on one wall, and a big mahogany desk in front of a bank of windows that opened on a terrace. The desk had four phones on it, and a few unopened letters. A tall guy with a dark olive complexion and funny, sleepy eyes was standing near the desk. He looked exactly like a hood. I mean, hoods don't really look like what the movies make out. Except this guy did. He had on a dark suit with a white stripe in it, and he was wearing a dark blue shirt and a white tie. He also had a scar up near his eye, and I swear to God if he didn't look like he stepped out of a Warner Brothers feature! Judging by his dark looks and all, I figured he was the one called 'Turk.' I mean, a guy who looked the way this one did, you just didn't call him 'Blondie' or 'Pinky' or like that. He was Turk all right. I'd bet my life on it.

Another guy was sitting behind the desk, wearing a gray seersucker suit, neatly pressed, with a white handkerchief in the breast pocket. No mountain peaks on the handkerchief; just folded flat, the way they wear them now in the magazines. He had on a black knit tie, very slim. A little silver pin pierced the tie and held it to his shirt. There was no bulge under *his* handkerchief. He wore gold-rimmed glasses, and he looked a little bit like a bank teller.

He stood up politely the minute Celia entered the room. He put out his hand and smiled, and I saw a gold tooth off center in the front of his mouth, matching the gold-rimmed glasses. He came around the desk lightly, almost like a queer, except I knew right away he wasn't. He just walked as if he knew exactly where he was going, and he did it fast, but he didn't fly around the room, the way queers do. A queer comes into the room, it's like a jet plane has just taken off. I can spot them from the back, from the front, sidewards, upside down, I can spot them. Once I was sitting in a movie on 125th, the Grand if you know the neighborhood, and this pansy got funny with me, and I almost broke his jaw. Mr Carfon walked light, but you got the feeling he was a man.

'Ah, Andy,' he said, smiling, 'good to see you. And Celia . . . ' And here his voice got warm, as if he was her father and she had just come back from some fancy dame's college for the Christmas vacation ' . . . how are you, Celia?'

'Hello, Mr Carfon,' Andy said, taking his hand. They shook, and then Mr Carfon turned and politely said, 'Turk, I don't know if you've ever met Mrs Orelli. Celia, Turk Fenton.'

Turk looked like he was in some kind of daze. The more I looked at him, the more I figured he was a fugitive from *The Maltese Falcon* or something. 'Yeah, how'd you do?' he said, smiling, his teeth forming a big enamel trench across his dark face.

42

Celia nodded and smiled and then went to sit in a chair near Mr Carfon's desk, crossing her legs. The one thing Celia had, I mean except this crazy, wild, loose-hipped, long-legged, big-busted body, was class. She walked like a lady, and when she sat she crossed her legs as if she was expecting a cup of tea and a slice of pound cake, tucking her skirt around her nicely. She had good posture. It's important to me that a dame walks like a dame and sits like one and is proud of herself. Dames got a right to walk with their heads up, especially when they're pretty.

'Is this the boy I've been hearing so much about, Andy?' Mr Carfon said.

'This is him,' Andy answered. 'Mr Carfon, I'd like you to meet Frankie Taglio.'

Mr Carfon stuck out his hand, and I took it. 'Frankie Taglio, is that right?' he said, pronouncing the name as if he was born in Milan.

'That's right,' I said.

'Taglio. Doesn't that mean "cut" in Italian?'

'Tell you the truth, I don't know,' I said.

'Well, no matter. I understand you know how to use a .45, Frankie.'

'Mr Carfon – '

'We can always use good men. Some of our best possibilities come from the street gangs. A man who shows himself to advantage in the street gangs is a made man.' He paused. 'I haven't heard your name associated with the clubs, Frankie.'

'I don't believe in that kid crap,' I said.

Mr Carfon smiled. 'And I don't believe in the use of profanity, however mild, in the presence of a lady.'

'I'm sorry,' I said.

'Certainly. Why don't you believe in the clubs?'

'What's the percentage? I don't see any kicks in stomping another guy into the sidewalk. The clubs are for kids.'

'I see. Well, in any case, Andy tells me he's checked on you, and you look like a good man. Now Andy's word is good enough for me. Oh, he's made a few mistakes every now and then, but on the whole he's a good man himself, and there's plenty of room for good men. How much are you earning now, Frankie?'

Before I could answer, Celia took a cigarette from her purse and started to fumble around for matches. Mr Carfon saw her from the corner of his eye, snatched a silver cigarette lighter from the desk, moved to her in that quick, light way and lit the cigarette.

Celia blew out a wreath of smoke. 'Thanks,' she said.

'Not at all,' Mr Carfon answered. 'You're looking well, Celia. I'd forgotten how lovely you looked.'

'Thanks.'

Mr Carfon nodded and then walked back to the desk, sitting on the edge of it. 'How much are you earning now, Frankie?' he asked again.

'At the moment, I ain't working,' I said.

'Well, that's interesting,' Mr Carfon said. 'Would you be interested in a job? Starting at, let us say, fifty dollars a week?'

'That sounds pretty low,' I said, and Celia looked up at me, surprised.

'Does it?' Mr Carfon asked.

'I can make that in the A&P.'

'How much did you have in mind, Frankie?'

'I had in mind all I can get,' I told him.

'All you can get is seventy-five to start, and that's tops. You can also get a little free advice against being overly ambitious.'

'What am I supposed to do for this seventy-five a week?'

'Lots of little things.' He smiled. 'Lord knows there're always a million little things to do, isn't that right, Turk?'

'Always,' Turk said, his eyes still sort of blank.

'We have a large organization, please don't misunderstand me. I wouldn't want to give the impression that you'd be doing these little things all by yourself. Do you see?'

'What *kind* of little things?' I asked.

'I see you believe in specifics. I take this to be a sign of intelligence, which is always good. Very well, I shall become specific. We have a warehouse deal on the schedule for tonight. We can use another man on it. If you're interested, of course.'

'What *kind* of warehouse deal?' I asked.

'I promised specifics, and I did not deliver them, did I? I do not ordinarily encourage too many questions, but I can see you're a cautious man. I'll spell it out for you, Frankie. You should, after all, know exactly what you're getting into – though I imagine you've already grasped at least part of it. We are going to break into and enter a warehouse. We are going to commit burglary. The warehouse has recently received a shipment of furs. We are going to steal those furs. And later we are going to sell them. That is the long and the short of it, Frankie. Are you interested?'

'This is the kind of little thing I'd be doing, right?'

'Exactly.'

'For seventy-five bucks a week, right?'

'Yes.'

I shook my head. 'At that salary, the A&P is safer. I want a hundred a week.'

'Seventy-five is as far as I'll go,' Mr Carfon said. 'And I'm not ready to enter a bargaining duel and then settle for eighty-five or ninety. Seventy-five is the salary, take it or leave it.' He smiled. 'Turk, ask Milt to get us something to drink, won't you? I don't want Frankie to think we're inhospitable. As I told you, Frankie, this is a big organization. But I don't need motivational research to teach me there's no percentage in treating the bottom men like animals. I don't believe in that. There's plenty of room at the top, and I don't want someone in command to bear a grudge in remembrance of shabby treatment he may once have received. Do you understand?'

'Yes, I understand. A hundred dollars is my price.'

'Have a drink first. Think about it. Turk?'

'I'll talk to Milt,' Turk said, and he walked out of the room. When he was gone, Mr Carfon turned to Celia. 'What do *you* think of Frankie here?' he asked.

'I think he has potential,' Celia said.

'Ah, yes, and I've always admired your good judgment. Do you own a gun, Frankie?'

'No.'

'You prefer a .45, I gather. We'll get you one.'

'I didn't take the job yet.'

'True, nor am I trying to high-pressure you. I think you'll find our organization worth while, though.'

'Am I expected to do any more killing?' I asked.

'Well now, that's certainly to the point, isn't it? Murder, eh? Well, I'll be honest with you. Perhaps. Perhaps you may have to kill again. Do you find the thought disagreeable?'

'Well . . . no,' I said cautiously.

'Then what is it?'

'I just wouldn't like it to become a habit. Not for a measly seventy-five bucks a week.'

'No, we habitually try to steer away from violence. Except where it is absolutely necessary, of course.' He smiled. 'And then we rise to meet the demands of the occasion.'

'I see.'

'So? What do you say?'

'I say I'll take the seventy-five a week . . . provided.'

'Provided what?'

'Provided it goes up to a hundred within a month. And provided the salary doubles the day I'm asked to kill anybody.'

Mr Carfon smiled. 'Very well,' he said, and I was already beginning to congratulate myself on being a shrewd business-man when he added, 'You'll join us in a drink, won't you? And then you can leave.'

'What?'

'Your counter-offer was unacceptable,' Mr Carfon said, still smiling. 'But that's the way it goes.' He shrugged.

'Well . . . '

'Think it over, Frankie,' Celia said.

I looked at her. I was beginning to kick myself for playing it so shrewd. The guy's offer had been a reasonable one.

'Well, Mr Carfon – ' I started.

'Ah, here's Milt and Turk with refreshments,' Mr Carfon said. 'Come in, boys.'

Milt came over with a tray full of drinks, serving Celia first. Mr Carfon said, 'Drink up, Frankie.'

We all drank. Then Mr Carfon said, 'Well, Frankie, it was very nice meeting you. I'm sorry it didn't work out between us, but that's the way the Tootsie rolls. If you'll excuse me now . . . '

'Mr Carfon . . . ?'

'Yes?'

'I'll . . . uh . . . I've been thinking.'

'Have you?'

'Yes. I'll . . . I'll take the job. For the seventy-five.'

'Seventy-five?' Mr Carfon said, still smiling. 'There must be some misunderstanding. The starting salary is fifty.'

'Fifty? But you said – '

'I said fifty,' Mr Carfon said, still smiling.

'Fifty,' I repeated, and then I nodded because I saw what had happened, and I had nobody to blame but myself. 'Okay,' I said. 'Fifty.'

'Good, I'm glad you're with us.' He took my hand and shook it. 'Celia, you may go now or as soon as you like. I want Frankie to stay so that Andy can explain tonight's job to him. I wouldn't want him to foul up his first time out.'

'I'm going tonight?' I asked.

'Yes, certainly. On the warehouse job.'

'Oh,' I said. 'Sure.'

Mr Carfon began walking Celia to the door, anxious to get her out now that the cordialities were done with. He put his arm around Celia's waist, and I heard him say, 'You're really looking quite lovely, Celia. You must come to see us more often.'

Milt, standing just inside the door, patted Celia on the behind again before she went out. Celia didn't seem to mind.

Andy didn't seem to notice.

4

The warehouse was a big monster on the lower West Side, near the West Side Highway. We drove up to it with our headlights off, and way up the Hudson on the other side, we could see the lights of Palisades; and while we were parking the heap, the boat coming back from Bear Mountain drifted by, and we could hear people singing out on the river.

There were four of us in the car. A guy whose name I didn't catch was driving. On his right, a small guy who'd been introduced as Weasel that afternoon sat chewing on a matchstick. Andy and I sat in the back seat. The deal had been explained very carefully by Andy that afternoon. He had a floor plan of the warehouse, and he knew just where everything was, including the alarm system. Weasel was the alarm expert, he told me. There wasn't an alarm in the world that Weasel couldn't foul up in ten minutes, Andy said. I hoped he was right.

The warehouse was surrounded by a cyclone fence which Andy said wasn't wired. There was a gate in the fence about fifteen feet back from the rear brick wall of the building. A ramp went through that gate and up to the loading platform at the back of the warehouse. The gate was held closed by a heavy padlock. There were two watchmen inside the building, and each one carried a key to the gate.

We pulled up close to the corner, on the blind wall of the building. The driver and Weasel stayed in the car. Andy and I went out. They had given me a .45, and I had the gun tucked in the waistband of my pants, and it felt very big and very hard against my belly. I stationed myself on the corner where I could see in all directions. The car was parked about twenty-five feet from me, the back doors open in case we had to make a run for it. Andy worked on the fence for about fifteen minutes, using a pair of heavy wire cutters. I kept watching for cops. I got to admit I was sweating. Finally, Andy came up to me and whispered, 'All right, get Weasel.'

I walked back to the car, not making any noise. It may sound stupid that we were wearing sneakers, but that's what we were wearing. Andy explained that Mr Carfon did things right, and sneakers don't make any noise on the floors of a warehouse.

I reached into the front open window and tapped Weasel on the shoulder. He opened the door and came out of the car. The car was a new Buick, and you could hardly even hear the engine, even though you knew it was running, purring under that long, sleek hood. We walked to the hole Andy had cut in the fence. Weasel squeezed through, and I squeezed in after him. Andy, because he was too fat to get through the hole, took up the sidewalk post, and began working on the fence some more, enlarging the hole. I wanted to pull out my gun and hold it in my hand, but Andy's gun was still in his shoulder holster, and I didn't want to seem chicken. I followed Weasel to where he knew the alarm wiring was, and then I walked around the side of the building and looked up to the catwalk I'd seen on the floor plan. There was a door on the second story of the building, opening onto the catwalk, and if a watchman showed, it would be through that door. I ducked into the shadows and kept my eyes on the door.

Andy had explained to me that afternoon a little about the kind of electric alarm systems used today. There was, he explained, the open circuit, the closed circuit and a combination of the two. The open circuit was the kind used by cheapskates who only wanted to make believe they had alarm protection. With that type of system, the alarm sounds when the circuit is closed, and you can put it out of action merely by cutting the wiring.

In the closed circuit kind of alarm, which is a little more expensive than the other, there's always a small current running through the wires, and the bells go off when you break that current in contact. The way you beat this alarm is by cross-contacting.

The warehouse we were hitting had the best type alarm, and

that was a combination of the other two kinds of alarms which went off either when the current was broken or when contact was made. There was only one way to beat this, and Weasel was working on that now. Actually, the wiring box was in a pretty stupid exposed place. The wiring is the weakest part of any alarm system, and some places bury it in concrete or under the floor or something. But this one was right where you could get at it and unscrew the lid to the box. When I went around to see how Weasel was coming along, he'd already laid open the wiring and was using a compass to find out which wires were carrying current. I went back to my post. Andy had already come through the bigger hole he'd cut in the unwired fence and had gone down to the gate where the padlock hung on the inside. He started working on the padlock while Weasel cross-contacted the wires carrying current and then cut the remaining wires. By the time Weasel finished with the alarm, Andy had the padlock open, too. For all practical purposes, the warehouse was now wide open.

Andy moved away from the padlock and signaled to the driver of the car. Slowly, no rush involved, the driver pulled away from the curb and drove out of sight. Together, Andy, me and Weasel walked to where the catwalk hung to the second story of the building. I was the tallest, so I jumped up for the ladder, pulling it down. Weasel went up the ladder first. Andy followed him, and then came me. At the door, Weasel checked for maybe a second wiring system, nodded, and then moved aside for Andy to work on the lock. He was really a whiz with locks, this Andy. He cracked the door in about thirty seconds, I'll swear it, and then he put his ear close to it and listened. According to what we knew, neither of the two watchmen should have been on the second floor at that time, but Andy was just making sure. He listened for a long time, and then he got ready to pull open the door. We all held our breaths. If Weasel had goofed even slightly, you'd be able to hear that alarm away the hell over in California. Andy pulled open the door.

The alarm didn't go off. Weasel smiled a little. It was so damn quiet on that catwalk, I could hear my old man's ghost breathing. Andy kept listening, even now with the door open. Then he nodded at Weasel and they both went inside while I watched the sidewalk. I was scared. I was goddamn good and scared. My hands were sweating, and my face was sweating, and my shirt was soaked through even though it was a pretty cool night.

'Come on,' Andy whispered, and I followed him into the building and eased the door shut behind me.

There were high walls all around us, and high windows on three of those walls. The fourth wall was a blind wall, big and blank, like a dummy's face. There were refrigerators all over the place. Everywhere you looked, you saw another refrigerator. There was enough refrigerators there to cool off all Africa.

We knew the furs were on the third floor, so we didn't have to say anything to each other. We'd worked this all out beforehand in the afternoon. We knew that one of the watchmen would be down on the first floor at this time, while the second watchman would be making his rounds. Weasel slipped away from us and darted downstairs after the first watchman. Andy and I started up for the third floor.

There were iron rungs on the steps to the third floor, and I imagined what leather soles would have done to those rungs. It would have been just like another alarm; only one you couldn't cut the wires on it. I was all at once very happy to be wearing sneakers. That's what I liked about the whole setup, the planning. We'd estimated the job for an hour and ten minutes, complete. We figured it would take us about a half-hour to get into the place and quiet the watchman, and another forty minutes to get the furs downstairs to the loading platform. That was a long time to be inside the place, but there were a lot of furs, and even with all that time we couldn't hope to load but a small percentage of them. But Andy explained that Mr Carfon was a very careful worker, and he worked on a very big scale. So if the job netted him only forty or fifty grand with just a portion of the furs, it was still a lot safer than using a truck and sticking around for the whole load, which maybe could have netted him two hundred grand, I don't know. That was the way Mr Carfon worked – safe. An hour and ten minutes, no more. At the end of that time, we would leave the building, no matter how many

51

furs we stacked. I suppose, if you looked at it another way, you could figure since you're already in the damn building, since you already took the risk, why not go all the way, why not absolutely clean it out? But Mr Carfon figured there was a point of diminishing returns, the way Andy put it, and since he had a big organization, he could afford to make a lot of smaller, safer heists.

He took no real chances. That was why the car had driven away. Now maybe that could be considered risky, leaving us inside the warehouse without a getaway car waiting. But if a Snow White happened to be cruising by, they'd sure as hell be suspicious of a car idling downstairs. I knew the car would be back a half-hour before our time was up, and that we'd have the first load of furs downstairs by that time. I knew the driver – what the hell was his name? – would open the gate and drive right up the ramp to the loading platform. I knew his lights would be out, and that we'd load the furs in complete darkness. I knew all that, and I felt pretty safe, but at the same time I couldn't help feeling a little scared.

The third floor was just like the second floor, minus the refrigerators. There were furs up there instead. The furs were on plain pipe racks, like Robert Hall advertises. We stood on the landing and looked through the open door. Our eyes were used to the darkness by this time, and we kept them peeled for the second watchman. Only we didn't see him anyplace on the floor.

'Where is he?' I whispered.

'He'll be around,' Andy said. 'Keep cool.'

We stayed on the landing for a good seven minutes. We heard Weasel starting up from the first floor, and then we didn't hear him all the way up to the third because of his sneakers.

When he came up to us, he said, 'I put him away and tied him up. Where's yours?'

'He hasn't showed yet,' Andy said.

Weasel glanced at the fluorescent dial of his watch. 'He better hurry,' he whispered. 'That car's gonna be back soon.'

'Maybe we should start taking the furs down,' I said.

'No,' Andy told me. 'We'll wait for the watchman.'

We kept waiting. I could hear Weasel's watch ticking away. I wondered if the car was back yet and waiting by the ramp down-stairs. Suppose a squad car spotted that car waiting?

'Where the hell is he?' I said.

'Cool, man,' Andy said.

'Suppose he stumbles on the guy Weasel put away? Suppose – ?'

'I said *cool*, man,' Andy snapped.

I listened to Weasel's watch, and I listened to my own breath-ing. The warehouse was very quiet, and the quiet mushroomed up like a hydrogen bomb, like if you ever watched the hydrogen bomb on television with the volume turned down, just like that. I could feel the sweat oozing down my back, and all at once I wanted that .45 in my hand. I reached under my jacket and pulled the gun out of my waistband. It made a scratching noise when it came free. Andy glanced at me and the gun, and then went back to watching the floor.

'He's probably taking a leak,' he said. 'He'll be around.' But he didn't sound so sure any more. I was thinking of the first watchman laying tied up downstairs, and I was wondering what would happen if our boy ran across him. I was wondering that and listening to the big silence and the steady tick of Weasel's watch, and I almost didn't hear the footsteps until Andy nudged me with his elbow.

He didn't say a word. He just nudged me, and I started listening, and then I heard the regular beat of heavy shoes on the concrete. I wiped my hand across my mouth, drying it, and then I wet my lips again with my tongue. The .45 was very heavy. I could feel my hand sweating against the checked stock. I listened to the footsteps coming closer and closer, and then Andy nudged me again, and when I looked at him he just made a sort of pulling gesture with his hand, telling me I should take the watchman.

I waited until the watchman passed the open landing door, and then I stepped out onto the floor behind him. He was an old man, and he walked with his head bent, his keys dangling from his right hand. He had a gun strapped to his waist, but the holster hung on his right side, and I knew his right hand was occupied with the keys. I stepped up behind him and threw my

53

left arm around his neck, thinking I'd pull him off balance and then hit him with the butt of the .45.

But maybe the old guy had seen better days, or maybe he'd been conked from behind before. Whatever the story, I didn't get a chance to yank him back toward me because he slipped his head out of my elbow lock and dropped to the floor like a tiger waiting to jump. At the same time, he dropped the keys, and his right hand went to his holster, and before I knew what was happening, there was a gun looking up at my face.

I could see the watchman's eyes, and those eyes were pale blue and slitted, hanging like narrow oysters on either side of his thin nose. His mouth was just a razor slash under that nose, and the face was altogether a mean sonovabitching face, and I knew he'd as soon shoot me as spit at me. I thought of the car waiting downstairs, and I kept looking from his gun to his face, and all of a sudden it was like just the two of us were left in the whole world, just the watchman and me, both of us waiting for something to happen, both of us maybe a little scared by what we knew was going to happen, but waiting for it anyway, and tensing for it, and sweating because of it.

'What are you doing here?' the watchman said, and I fired.

The bullet took him smack between the eyes. There were just the pale blue oyster slits, and then a hole popped up between the slits, like a blob of ketchup, and the old man pitched forward on his face. The sound of the explosion echoed around the high room, and then Andy was standing next to me on one side, and Weasel was on the other side, and they both started to talk at once, but all I heard was Andy saying like a hysterical woman, 'What the frig'd you do? What the frig'd you do?'

'I . . . I shot him,' I said.

'You dumb bastard,' Weasel said.

'Let's get out of here,' I said. 'Come on, let's get out of here.'

'Stay where you are,' Andy said. 'Don't move a friggin' muscle.'

We stayed where we were. I could see the old man's blood spreading in a circle on the floor under his head. I watched the blood spread, and when it almost touched my sneaker, I moved back. We didn't say a word to each other. We just stood there and listened and after a long while, Andy whispered, 'All right, let's load the furs.'

'You mean . . . '

'We came after the furs,' Andy said. 'I don't think the shot was heard. Let's load them.'

We walked over to the nearest rack, and Andy loaded Weasel's arms, and Weasel started downstairs. When it came time to load my arms, Andy said, 'Put that friggin' cannon away. You done enough damage with it already.'

I tucked the gun in my waistband and then held my arms out while Andy piled on the furs. The furs felt very warm and very soft. I carried them down to the loading ramp on the first floor. Weasel had the doors open, and the Buick was backed to the doors, with the trunk gaping open. I tossed the furs inside and then followed Weasel upstairs for another load. I wasn't scared so much now. I wasn't even sweating any more.

We worked quiet and fast. We packed the trunk solid, and then we closed it and started packing the back seat and floor of the car. We left room for one guy to sit back there, and when we filled the back, we covered the stuff with a blanket and then took off. We didn't bother closing the platform doors, and we didn't close the gate in the cyclone fence.

I sat in the back with the furs, and my hand under the blanket rested on one of the minks, and the touch was like some kind of a charge. I kept thinking of minks and Caddys, and I wondered how Celia would look in a mink, and when we drove up onto the parkway, I looked over to Palisades and wondered if Celia had ever been on a roller coaster. The idea of her screaming on a roller coaster, hanging onto me, her blonde hair blowing over her shoulders, was exciting. I didn't think about the dead watchman at all. Until Weasel started chewing me out.

'You're a little trigger-happy, you know, man?' he said.

'Who, me?' I said.

'No, the man in the moon. Who the hell do you think I mean? Who shot the watchman, if not you?'

'He had a gun,' I said. 'He would've shot me.'

'You're lucky we didn't get the whole damn police force down around our ears.'

'I heard the shot downstairs,' the driver said. 'I figured the job was through when I heard that.'

'He was going to shoot me,' I said. 'You didn't see that bastard's eyes. I bet he's shot more guys than I got toes.'

'Yeah, that's *your* story,' Weasel said.

'You saw he had a gun, didn't you?'

'That don't mean he was going to shoot.'

'No? What was he gonna do with it, then? Pick his nose?'

'Mr Carfon ain't gonna like this,' Weasel said. 'He don't like sloppy jobs.'

'What was sloppy about it?' I said. 'We got the furs, didn't we?'

'We also left a dead man.'

'What the hell, he was going to shoot me! Am I supposed to stand around and just get shot?'

'You're trigger-happy,' Weasel said.

'Look, I already been shot once, thanks, and I don't want no more holes in me. If a guy's ready to plug me, am I supposed to stand around and sing "The Star-Spangled Banner"? That's for the birds, man.'

'The watchman was scared crapless,' Weasel said. 'He wasn't going to shoot.'

'That's what you say. You was safe on the landing. How the hell do you know what he would or wouldn't have done? I'd have been the one got shot, not you. What the hell do you care how I bleed?'

'Don't get snotty with me, punk,' Weasel said. 'I pick my teeth with punks like you.'

'That's what the watchman thought, too,' I said, and all at once the car was very quiet. I listened to the silence, and I wondered if they were scared of me, and just wondering it made me feel a little like a big shot.

'Well,' Weasel said, backing off, 'don't be so trigger-happy. Mr Carfon don't like it.'

'If he don't like it,' I said, 'he can tell me so himself.' And that was the end of that.

We dumped the furs where we were supposed to, and then we split up, and I didn't get word from Mr Carfon until the next day. It was Andy who called me.

'Hello, Frankie,' he said. 'What are you doing?'

'I was sleeping.'

'Well, get some clothes on. I'll be over in about ten minutes.'

'What's the scoop?'

'Mr Carfon wants to see you.'

'Oh?'

'Yeah, make it snappy.'

I got dressed and waited for Andy, who came by in about a half-hour and not the ten minutes he promised. When I went down to the car, I was disappointed Celia wasn't with him, but then I realized she wouldn't be along with him every place he went. He didn't say a word on the drive downtown. We sat side by side like two dummies.

It was Turk Fenton who opened the door to Mr Carfon's place. He was wearing a blue gab that made my mouth water. He smiled his dopey kind of grin and then said, 'Come in, boys. Mr Carfon's tied up on a long-distance call, but he shouldn't be too long.' He took us into the living room, and then left us and went into Mr Carfon's office.

'What's his story?' I asked.

'No story,' Andy said.

'How come Celia didn't know him?'

'He's from Chicago,' Andy said. 'Him and Mr Carfon used to be in business together a long time ago. Mr Carfon felt he could use him in our operation, and so he sent for him. He's only been with us maybe three months.'

'He's a pretty big man, ain't he?'

'Sure.'

'I thought there was room at the top,' I said. 'If Mr Carfon needed somebody, how come he had to go outside the organization?'

'There *is* room at the top,' Andy said. 'And you ask too many questions.'

'How else you going to learn?' I said.

'Okay, then let me spell something simple. Mr Carfon took

Turk in because he needed help in Chicago. Turk is a *really* big man there. So if we get Turk, we also get what we need in the windy city. Clear?'

'Very clear. And do we have what we need now?'

'We have it.'

'Then why does he still hang on to Turk?'

'Turk's a good man.'

'He seems like he's in a fog.'

'Don't let him fool you. He's a shrewd operator.'

'I'm from Missouri,' I told him, and just then the door to Mr Carfon's office opened and he came out smiling.

'Hello, boys,' he said, and then he came over and shook hands with both of us, the gold tooth showing in his mouth, just off center. 'You don't mind if we sit here in the living room, do you? I've been on the telephone all morning, and a change is as good as a rest, they tell me.' He chuckled and then took a cigarette from a box on the coffee table. Andy started to light it for him, but Mr Carfon sort of pooh-poohed him aside and lit his own cigarette.

'Now then, Frankie,' he said, and he turned to me and smiled for just a second, and then the smile dropped from his mouth, the gold tooth turned off like a busted neon sign. 'Tell me about last night.'

'We got the furs,' I said.

'That's not what I want to know.'

'Well, what do you want to know?'

'I should have thought you'd learned by now that a person who fences with me is liable to get cut. Surely, Frankie, we can have a conversation without this senseless parry and thrust.'

'All right,' I said. 'I shot the watchman.'

'Yes. Why?'

'He was going to shoot me.'

'How do you know?'

'He had a gun in his hand, and the gun was pointed at me. I don't think people point guns unless they plan to shoot.'

'Dubious reasoning,' Mr Carfon said. 'Did you stop to consider what far-reaching consequences your impetuous act might have brought?'

'I don't know what you mean,' I said. I really didn't.

'Do you realize,' Mr Carfon said slowly, 'that cooling the watchman could have brought the police down on our asses?'

'No.'

'Well, start using that frigging head of yours,' Mr Carfon said. 'I told you I don't go for unnecessary bloodshed. I also seem to recall a certain displeasure on your part concerning the entire subject of wanton killing. Your stand seems to have reversed itself. If you are now intent on using that gun of yours, we'll see that you get plenty of opportunity. But not on a simple caper like the one last night. Is that clear?'

'It was self-defense,' I said.

'Is that clear?' Mr Carfon said.

'It was self-defense,' I repeated.

Mr Carfon moved over to me with that quick, light motion, reaching down for my lapels and pulling me off the couch. He held me right close to his face and he said, 'I asked you a question, Frankie. I asked if you understood what I was telling you. I asked if it was entirely clear in your mind. I expect an answer.'

'What was the question?' I said.

Mr Carfon suddenly slapped me. He kept holding my lapels in one hand, and the other hand lashed out and caught me on the right cheek.

'Hey . . .'

'Go ahead, reach for your gun,' Mr Carfon said.

'I wasn't going to reach for no gun.'

'That's smart,' Mr Carfon said. 'Now just remember that you're not to reach for a gun ever, unless you're told to. Or unless it's perfectly clear that your life or the welfare of any particular caper is at stake. Is that clear?'

'Yes, that's clear.'

'If you want to use a gun, we've got a lot of little jobs that require one. Isn't that so, Turk?'

'A lot of little jobs,' Turk said, nodding stupidly.

'Why don't you let go my coat?' I said to Mr Carfon.

For a minute, I thought he was going to slap me again. He looked as if he was trying to decide. Finally, he let go of my lapels and smiled. I'll tell you the truth, it's a good thing he did. Because I was pretty pissed off by this time, and if he'd have slapped me one more time, I'd have slugged him and then mopped up the floor with every son of a bitch in the room. I don't like being pushed around, and bigger guys than Mr Carfon have tried it and found out Frankie Taglio don't take nothing from nobody.

'You've got spirit,' he said dryly. 'I think it might be a mistake to break that spirit.'

'It might be a big mistake,' I said, because I was still pissed off and I was just about getting ready to walk out on Mr Carfon and his big-shot organization that took care of the man on the bottom by slapping him around.

'You're new in this business,' Mr Carfon said.

'That's right,' I told him. I was real sore now, and he could see it.

'You're not stupid, Frankie. I know you'll understand me when I say it doesn't pay to have trouble over a few thousand dollars. Last night's caper was a very simple thing, and it shouldn't have involved a killing. When corpses are necessary, you'll know about it. But they are *not* necessary on a penny-ante deal. Would you like a cigarette?'

'All right,' I said, but I said it nasty so he'd know I was still sore and wasn't going to be taken in by all this buddy-buddy crap. He handed me the cigarette box, and I took one, and then he lit it for me.

'And do we understand each other, Frankie?'

'We understand each other real fine,' I said.

'If you like to use your gun – '

'I didn't say I like to – '

'If you *like* to use your gun,' he said over my voice, 'we'll see that you use it. But let us decide when and where it's to be used.'

I didn't say anything.

'Please,' Mr Carfon added, and he smiled politely.

'Okay,' I said.

'We are agreed?'

I shrugged, and then I smiled back. 'We are agreed,' I said.

'Good. On the whole, you did very well last night. I think you're going to work out fine. Now then, Andy?'

'Yes, Mr Carfon?'

'I've got a little errand for you. I hope you don't mind.'

'Not at all, Mr Carfon.'

'There's a drop on Lenox and 133rd. A man named Keller runs it. I suspect Mr Keller has been dipping into the till. I'd like you to talk to Mr Keller and advise him that such petty horse manure can very well lead to a fractured skull. Would you do that for me, Andy?'

'Certainly,' Andy said.

'I'd send Frankie along with you, just to watch, but I'd like him to get some new clothes. You do look rather shabby, Frankie, if you don't mind my saying so.' He chuckled. 'Not exactly Madison Avenue.' He chuckled again. 'Turk?'

'Yeah?'

'Give Frankie some money from petty cash, won't you? Several hundred should cover it. Frankie, need I send someone with you, or can I rely on your inherent good taste?'

'I think I can manage,' I said, smiling.

'Fine.' He turned to Andy. 'How long do you suppose you'll be with Mr Keller?'

'Hour or two. I don't know.'

'No rough stuff, Andy. Just a friendly chat. Will you call me when you're through?'

'Sure.'

'Use the private number, will you?'

'All right. Just one thing, Mr Carfon.'

'What's that?'

'Well, after I talk to Keller. Was there anything else? I was planning on maybe going to a ball game this afternoon.'

'Go right ahead.'

'Thanks,' Andy said. 'I'll go straight from Keller's place.'

'I won't need you at all today, Frankie,' Mr Carfon said. 'Get your clothes. I'll keep in touch with you.'

Turk handed me some loot, and I thanked him and stuck it in my pocket. I shook hands with Mr Carfon, and then me and Andy left.

Downstairs, Andy said, 'You want to meet me later, come along to the game?'

'No, I don't think so.'

'Gonna be a good game.'

'No. Thanks, anyway.'

'Well, what're you gonna do with your time?'

'Knock around. I'll find something to do.'

'Don't get in no trouble,' Andy said. 'You're going uptown, I'll give you a lift.'

'No, I think I'll head for the men's stores downtown.'

'Don't buy nothing loud,' Andy said. 'Mr Carfon don't like nothing loud. I'll see you.'

He walked to his car, and I watched him drive off, thinking about what he'd said. He'd kill an hour or two with Keller, and then he was going to the ball game. I could do all the shopping I had to do later. That would wait. For now, there was something else that had to be done.

I caught a cab and headed up to see Celia.

5

All the way uptown, I kept hoping she'd be home. And then I kept telling myself she wouldn't be home, just so I wouldn't be disappointed in case she wasn't. I used to play that game with myself when I was a kid. I remember one Christmas I was wishing so hard for a two-wheeler bike I almost got to be a nervous wreck. So I kept telling myself, 'You ain't gonna get that bike. You're gonna wake up Christmas morning, and there's gonna be the usual five-and-dime crap under the tree, and maybe some socks or ties from one of Papa's sisters. But no bike.' That's what I kept telling myself. And when Christmas morning came, there wasn't no bike, just like I really knew there wouldn't be. And I wasn't so disappointed, though I'll tell you the truth, it really broke my heart that Christmas morning.

I did the same thing to myself now. First I said, 'She'll be home,' and then I said, 'She won't.' Back and forth, like a ping-pong game. When the cab pulled up in front of her building, I reached into my pocket for the wad Turk had given me. There was five hundred dollars in that wad! I'd never seen so much money all together in all my life! I whistled and handed the cabbie a fiver, and then I pocketed the wad and climbed up the steps on the front stoop. Some kids were playing Johnny-on-a-Pony, and a skinny kid in the pony line was having a hell of a time holding up another kid who must have weighed at least four hundred pounds.

I went into the building and almost ran up to the third floor. I walked down to the door at the end of the hall, and I stopped to catch my breath, and I thought, *Be home, Celia honey. Please be home.* And then I thought, *She won't be home.*

I knocked on the door.

There was a long pause, and then I heard her say, 'Who is it?'

My hands were beginning to shake a little. 'Me,' I said. 'Frankie.'

'Oh.' She paused. 'Just a second.'

I waited for her to come to the door, wondering what she'd be wearing, hoping she'd have on what she had on the night she cleaned my leg. I wondered what it would be like when she let me into the apartment. I was getting very nervous in the hallway there. I've always been an impatient guy. If something's gonna happen, I like it to happen quick.

The door came back a little, and then was stopped by the chain. Celia's face showed in the crack of the door, the blonde hair hanging loose over one eye. She didn't have on no lipstick. I figured I'd rustled her out of bed.

'If you want Andy,' she said, 'he's not home.'

'I know. I don't want Andy.'

'No? What do you want?'

'You know what I want,' I said. 'Take the chain off the door.'

'Just like that, huh?' she said.

'Yes. Just like that.'

'Suppose I don't want to take the chain off?'

'You do. I know you do.'

'Andy may be home any minute,' she said. 'Andy's a very jealous man.'

'Andy's doing an errand for Mr Carfon. And after that he's going to a ball game. Andy *won't* be home any minute.'

'My,' Celia said, and I could see her smiling in the crack of the door. 'You've really planned this out, haven't you?'

'Haven't *you?*' I said. 'Take off the chain.'

'I'm not even dressed,' she said. 'I was taking a nap when you came.'

'Let me in, Celia,' I said.

'I told you. I'm not dressed.' She stepped a little closer to the door, and I could see the hint of white flesh showing in the narrow wedge between the door and the doorframe.

'Open it, Celia,' I said.

'Lower your voice,' she said, and I could see the smile on her mouth behind the goddamn thick wooden door that separated us. 'I have neighbors, you know.'

'I don't care about – '

'What would my neighbors think? A strange man calling on me when I'm not even dressed?'

'Open the door, Celia!'

'Do you really want me to open the door?'

'Yes, damnit!'

It was a funny thing. I mean, it was like that time in the car. That time it was as if holding her ankle was everything there was in the world. This time it was as if what was happening there with that door between us, with that damn chain keeping the door closed against me, with the glimpses of her body and her face and her blonde hair flashing into the wedge, it was as if this was everything there was. It was as if everything would have already happened the minute she took off the chain. After that, there maybe would be a letdown. This was the whole bit, the whole mounting, building goddamn bit to the minute she took off that chain and let me into the apartment.

'Won't you please go, Frankie?' she said poutingly.

'No.'

'But I told you, baby, I'm not *dressed*. You don't want to come in and find me this way, do you?'

'Yes. That's what I want, Celia.'

'If I took off this chain, Frankie, I'm not sure I'd be able to trust myself.'

'Take off the chain, Celia.'

'Oh, but Frankie, I'm afraid,' she said, and she didn't sound afraid at all. 'Suppose I lost control of myself? Suppose – '

'Open it, Celia!'

'Don't force me, Frankie!'

'Open the goddamn door!'

'Why? What do you want, Frankie?'

'You know what I want.'

'What?' she whispered. 'Tell me.'

'I want to go to bed with you.'

The hall was very quiet. In the wedge of the door, Celia was no longer smiling. Slowly, she wet her lips with her tongue, and then her hand came up, slowly, slowly, passing the white flesh of her breasts, the puckering thrust, and then the shadowed hollow of her throat, and then her slender fingers touched the metal and she took off the chain.

The streets were alive.

You can say what you want about New York, but it's the only city that jumps. It jumps twenty-four hours a day. It jumps in the morning when everybody's rushing to get to work, it jumps at lunchtime when everybody's in the streets rushing around digging everything, it jumps all afternoon when the kids are out of school and playing stickball or riding their pushos or playing stoopball or just lounging with the girls; it jumps, it's the goddamned jumpingest town in the world. And at night, when the lights come on, they set the pace, man, they tell the world this is New York, come live, man, this is New York where everybody's alive, where everybody jumps!

I was feeling great that afternoon. There were kids swarming all over the streets, and I could hear the honk of horns and that big groaning sound the buses make when they pull away from the curb, and the swish of the DSC trucks sprinkling the streets, and the yells of the guys selling fruit and vegetables from wagons that were still pulled by horses. I wished somebody would turn on a johnny pump because I felt like running right under the water with my clothes on. Jesus Christ, she was a woman. Jesus Christ, I was flying!

I walked along feeling like I owned the city. Everything in the city was mine, you follow me? I owned that skyline. It belonged to me, Frankie Taglio, and the hell with you! I owned those streets that cut like razors from the Hudson to the East River. I owned all those bridges that connected all the goddamn confused boroughs of the city, I owned everybody running around in the streets, I owned all the kids who were screaming their heads off, and I owned all the young girls who were just beginning to blossom, and I owned all the older girls in their tight dresses with their marvelous wiggling little behinds; I owned the streets, I owned the buildings, I owned the people, I owned the city!

I wanted more of her. I wanted all I could get.

I was still flying when I ran into May. I was walking down

Third Avenue, and for a minute I missed the El, did you ever feel that way? It was like I expected it to be there, and all of a sudden it wasn't there. I missed the shadow all at once, and the big noise of the trains and the sparks that used to fly down into the street. There was a big wide avenue now where the elevated used to be, and I was walking along thinking how everything changes and thinking how I myself was beginning to change in just the past few days, how I was on my way to being somebody in a big outfit, how if I played my cards right I could be a big man, when I ran into May.

'Frankie!' she said, and I stopped short and looked around for a few minutes, and then I saw her standing on the sidewalk near the furniture store.

'Oh, hello, May,' I said.

I walked over to her, and she smiled with all of her face, the way she always smiled, her eyes crinkling and her nose crinkling and her lips opening over the whitest teeth God ever made. I got to explain the way May looked that day because I think it was a part of this feeling that I owned the city. I felt, you see, like I owned her too a little. I guess it tied in with what happened with Celia, but Celia was something you did, and May could be something you owned, I don't know if that makes any sense. But anyway she was wearing a bright yellow dress, a sort of cotton thing, I guess. It looked very good on her because of the black hair cut real close to her head and the big brown eyes which always looked to me like the kind of eyes you expect on some South Sea Island girl, sort of tilted, you know, and fringed with very thick black lashes. She was a pretty kid, May, with none of the kind of electricity that came out of Celia, but Celia was an older woman, thirty, you know, and May was only nineteen and with this sweetness coming out of her, like a young, pure thing you wanted to pet. I hadn't seen her since before that night I got shot, and it was good seeing her again. I mean it.

'Where have you been, Frankie?' she said.

'Oh, around.'

'You haven't called.'

'No. I been busy.'

'Too busy to pick up a telephone?'

'Yeah, I've been real busy.'

'It was kind of sudden, you know. All at once, no Frankie. You date me three months in a row, and then you can't even afford a phone call.'

'I can afford phone calls.'

'Then why didn't you call me?'

'I told you. I was busy.'

'Are you still busy?'

'Yes.'

'Oh.'

'That ain't what I meant. Look, May, I got to go downtown. I'll give you a ring, huh?' I don't know why, but she was beginning to give me a sort of pressed feeling. It started out with me feeling I owned her, and now it was twisting around so that I wanted to get clear fast before she owned me. 'I'll give you a ring, huh?'

She opened the brown peepers wide and nailed them right to my eyes and said, 'When?'

I had to laugh. She looked so damn cute in that minute that I forgot all about being owned. 'Boy, you don't believe in rushing a guy, do you?'

'When the guy is you, it makes a difference,' she said. 'I was very hurt when you stopped calling, Frankie.'

'Well,' I said, 'I was out of town for a while. That's why I didn't call, you see.'

'Really? Where were you?'

'Just out of town.'

'Vacation?'

'Sort of.'

We didn't say anything for a few minutes. I didn't know whether to ask her out or not. I thought of Celia and how different they were from each other, but of course Celia was something else, I mean I didn't even *think* of taking Celia out, I mean that was out of the question.

'What are you doing now?' I said.

'You mean right this minute?'

'Yeah, sure.'

'Nothing special. I was just . . .' She stopped. 'Why?'

'You want to come downtown with me? I got some shopping to do.'

'What kind of shopping?'

'A few shirts, a suit, things like that. What do you say? You can help me pick them out.'

'Well . . . I don't know . . .'

'And we can get a bite to eat and take in a show later. What do you say?'

May smiled. 'I'd love it, Frankie,' she said.

I began seeing Celia every night Andy was away.

September had just rolled in, and there ain't none of this falling-leaves jive in the city; there's just the feeling that life's about to begin, everybody's kicking off that old summer dust and getting ready to come to grips with that bastard winter again. It was great. I really felt great. Having Celia was like having an oil well in Texas.

One night, one of those crazy cool nights, I was dressing when the phone rang. I went out of the bedroom and into the living room. I picked up the phone and said, 'Yah?'

'Is that a way to answer the phone?' Celia said.

'Celia? Hey, I'm sorry, I thought . . . I was expecting . . .'

'One of your other women, I guess,' Celia said.

'No, Milt.'

'Can you come over tonight?'

'What?'

'Tonight. Andy's not going to be home. Can you come here?'

'Well . . .'

'Don't you want to?'

'Oh, baby, how I want to.'

'Then?'

'I can't. There's a big meeting at Mr Carfon's place.'

'You don't have to go.'

'Sure I do. You know that. I have to go.'

'Break it, Frankie. Come to me.'

'Celia, I can't.'

She sighed, and that sigh went through me like a spear, I swear it. 'Tomorrow night then?' she said. 'I'll get rid of Andy.'

'What time?'

'Eight o'clock. I'll send Andy to the fights.'

'Gone,' I said.

'Good. I'll be waiting. Good-bye, boy.'

I hung up and smiled. My mother looked up at me. She was wearing an old house dress, and she had that drunkard's look on her face, you know the look I mean? Where all the respect goes, and where there's nothing left but a pair of sad eyes and a droopy mouth, where even the skin seems to have given up the fight.

'You going out again, Frankie?' she said.

'Yeah.' I went over to her, and I sat down next to her, feeling sorry for her all at once. 'Ma,' I said, 'why don't you lay off that stuff, huh?'

'Leave me alone, Frankie,' she told me. 'Don't tell your mother what to do.'

'Ma, listen to me. I'm going places. I'm gonna be a big man, I mean it. You don't have to . . . to poison yourself like this. Look, Ma, in a little while maybe we can get out of this dump, you know? Get out of Harlem for good, you see? I'll be able to get you nice clothes, and a good house, and a car maybe. How'd you like that, Ma? A nice car.'

'I don't want a nice car,' she said.

'Come on, Ma, can't you just lay off this stuff? Ma, it's only . . . Ma, don't you remember what you used to look like, how you used to walk, and laugh, and be fun all the time? Ma, for Christ's sake, can't you – ?'

'Oh, shut up!' she said.

I got up and went out of the room, and when I was tying my tie I all of a sudden felt like crying. What was the sense? I thought. What the hell was the sense of anything? The Russians are ready to grab outer space, and my mother is a drunken pig. What's the sense?

I sat in the bedroom all alone, wearing my new suit, smoking a cigarette, waiting for Milt to call. In the living room, my mother began weeping the way she always does when the sauce takes hold of her, crying for ghosts, crying for dead things, not knowing she herself was a ghost. Milt called and said he'd stop by for me at seven thirty. When he got there at seven twenty-five, my mother was passed out on the couch. He took a look at her, but he didn't say nothing. Nobody has to say nothing about a drunk. A drunk is a drunk. You just don't spell it any other way.

Milt was driving a big new Olds. We piled in, and he said, 'Big doings tonight.'

'Yeah? How so?'

'You'll see.'

'We got to do another caper?'

'No, nothing like that. You'll see.'

He was smiling like that disappearing cat in the *Alice in Wonderland* thing, and I wondered just what *was* up. I knew Milt was a pretty big man because, as far as I could see, he never went out on a caper. The way I figured it, there was Mr Carfon who was the top and untouchable. Then there was Turk Fenton who was sort of like Mr Carfon's confidential assistant, although maybe he was a full partner, having brought in the Chicago crowd.

The organization branched out after that into a lot of little organizations, like sort of branch offices with one executive office. Milt, Andy, Weasel, Jobbo, me, and about half a dozen other guys formed one branch of the organization. I'd met a few guys from the other branches, like the Bronx crowd, and the Nassau County bunch, and even once a guy from some hick town named Monticello, but of course I wasn't real chummy with them.

Milt was like the top man in our branch. He took orders from nobody but Mr Carfon and Turk. Then came Andy, I supposed, and then Weasel, and I was on a par with Jobbo and the other half-dozen guys – or maybe I was just a little ahead of them, who knows? Truth was, I hardly saw Jobbo at all since the night I got shot, so maybe he wasn't even a part of the thing, maybe he just was what Turk called a punk. But I *was* a part of the thing, that's for sure, a big outfit and a very smooth-running one, with plenty room for advancement because guys were always being promoted. It sounds funny when you say it like that, but that's just the way it worked – like a big business outfit.

71

Andy and Weasel and Petey and Max and Carrie and most of the guys from our branch were there when we got to Mr Carfon's place. I didn't see Turk around noplace, but I figured he was in back with Mr Carfon. There were drinks around, so I helped myself, and I munched on some potato chips and such, and just shot the breeze with the boys. Andy was in a pretty chipper mood, it seemed, and when Milt asked him 'How's that piecy wife of yours, man?' he just smiled and chuckled and nodded his head, and I thought, Man, if you only knew how that piecy wife of yours *really* is! Anyway, everybody seemed to be in a real happy mood, so I figured something happy was in the breeze. Maybe Mr Carfon was going to give us a bonus or something.

After about ten minutes, Mr Carfon came out of his office.

'Hello, boys,' he said. 'Are we all here?'

'We're all here, Mr Carfon,' Milt said, and he smiled that big smile again. Well, we weren't all there because I still didn't see Turk anywhere around, but I guess I was the only guy who noticed this, so I kept my mouth shut.

'Think the host can get something to drink?' Mr Carfon said, and the boys all laughed. Andy brought Mr Carfon a Scotch and soda, and he drank a little of it, and then walked around chatting with the boys, clapping Milt on the shoulder every now and then. I still didn't see Turk around, so I naturally figured Mr Carfon was waiting for him before he called the meeting to order. But along around nine o'clock, Mr Carfon cleared his throat and said, 'Well, boys, I'd like to make a little announcement.'

Milt smiled, and Andy smiled, and all the boys shut up and started paying attention to what Mr Carfon was saying.

'Starting now,' he said, 'starting right this minute, you'll be taking your orders equally from me and Milt Hordzig.'

Well, man, you could have knocked me down with a Mack truck! I looked at Milt, and he just stood there smiling ear to ear, and Andy was still smiling too, and I wondered just what the hell had become of Turk. Nobody was asking, though, so I figured I'd just better keep my mouth shut.

'Yes,' Mr Carfon went on, 'Milt is moving up. And because

he's moving up, Andy Orelli will move up, too. I thought you'd all like to know about it, and that's why I called you together tonight. Now, there won't be any more speeches. Drink, enjoy yourselves, and if there's anything you desire – I mean *any*thing – just see me or Milt about it.'

Well, the boys all began laughing it up, patting Milt and Andy on the back, congratulating them, and then hitting the bottles in earnest. We drank for a long time, getting happier and happier, with no one asking anything about Turk. But I'm like the cat, you know? I got a big curious nature. So I went over to Andy along about eleven o'clock or thereabouts, and I took him aside and said, 'What about Turk?'

'What about him?' Andy said thickly.

'He ain't been . . . you know?'

'No. He's still with the organization.'

'I don't get it.'

'He was on H,' Andy said.

'Heroin?'

'Mmm. And Mr Carfon found out. Mr Carfon don't like no hophead in the upper brackets.'

'Turk was a hophead?'

'From here to China and back,' Andy said.

'So that's no reason to dump him. I mean, hell, what about the Chicago bunch? You sure Mr Carfon did the right thing?'

'The Chicago bunch has been with Mr Carfon for the past six weeks. Turk was as necessary as a hole in the head. Besides, he's a junkie, and Mr Carfon don't like it. Period. That's all she wrote. Listen, I'm not complaining. This brings me up to three bills a week. Man, I'm tickled Turk digs heroin.'

'Yeah, but still – '

'Mr Carfon didn't like the idea,' Andy said, whispering now. 'There's a lot of things Mr Carfon don't like.'

Milt came reeling over to us. Man, he was stoned. Well, what the hell, it ain't every day you get to be a real big man. 'Wha's the matter?' he said. 'Wha's the matter?'

'Nothing,' Andy said. 'We was just talking.'

'But what happened to Turk?' I asked Andy. 'You said he was still in the organization.'

'Turk?' Milt said. 'You mean old Turk the hophead? Why sure Turk is still in the outfit. Why, didn't you know that, boy? Mr Carfon give him a choice. Mr Carfon said, "Now, Turk, we don't like hopheads around here in command posts. Now you got to go, Turk. Now if you're thinking you're gonna take all that Chicago bunch with you, you got another guess, Turk, because that Chicago crowd knows where that good bread is buttered and I got that whole crowd right in my pocket now. So I'm giving you a choice. You can go, and I mean really go, I mean go, man, good-bye – or you can take a job we find for you in the outfit someplace, where you can go on puffing that weed of yours and sticking that spike in your arm, but where you can't do no harm to nobody else in the outfit. Now which do you want, Turk? Which one? Take your choice." That's what Mr Carfon said.'

'So Turk took the job,' Andy said.

'Which job?'

Milt began laughing like an idiot. '*Which* job? A job in Chicago. Listen, what difference does it make? He's lucky he's still walking around. Mr Carfon must have been feeling kind. Listen, Turk's lucky they ain't pulling him out of the East River.'

'How come they ain't?' I said.

'He's a hophead,' Milt said. 'The outfit'll keep him on the junk, and he's like a vegetable. You ever try to hold a conversation with a vegetable? Impossible. Turk ain't gonna be talking to nobody. Besides, he's being watched. One false move – zing. Listen, did somebody call Angelo?'

'I called him,' Andy said.

'Did you tell him we want tall girls? I like tall girls,' Milt said.

'I told him tall girls.'

'Good man,' Milt said, and he clapped Andy on the shoulder.

The girls arrived maybe about a half-hour later. They were very tall girls. They were maybe the tallest girls I ever seen in my life. They got right in the swing of things. One thing about the girls Angelo got, you never felt they were sluts. I mean, these girls were all dressed very refined, and they began drinking like ladies, and then circulating around the room, just like ladies. It began to get a little rougher later on, of course. I mean, they weren't there to play bean bag. But even hanging around guys' necks or sitting on their laps, they still didn't look like sluts. That's what I liked about the girls Angelo got. I tell you the truth, I was getting a little bored with this redhead who was hanging around me. I was thinking of Celia, and how I'd see her tomorrow night. I guess it showed on my face. I ditched the redhead to get a drink.

'Are you enjoying yourself, Frankie?' I heard someone say.

I turned. Mr Carfon was standing at my elbow, smiling, the gold tooth gleaming.

'Sure, Mr Carfon,' I said. 'I'm having a swell time.'

'Good. I understand more entertainment will be here shortly.'

'Yes.' He was referring to a dancer who was supposed to come.

'I imagine you'll enjoy that.'

'Yes.'

'Good. You haven't been very active lately, have you, Frankie?'

'No, I ain't.'

'I've got something for you,' Mr Carfon said. 'For tomorrow night.'

'When?'

'Tomorrow night. A whisky shipment. It's so simple you could probably handle it alone. But Weasel and Carrie will go along with you.'

'Tomorrow night,' I said.

'Yes. Now listen to me, Frankie, and listen closely. Andy won't be going on any of these . . . ah . . . expeditions any more. Now, I certainly trust all the other boys, but they're lacking a little in the upstairs department, do you follow?' He tapped his temple with one finger. 'I can't entrust big things to men with small brains. Do you follow me?'

'Yes, Mr Carfon,' I said. I was wondering how I could break the news to Celia, how I could tell her about not being able to make it again tomorrow.

'You're a smart boy, Frankie,' Mr Carfon said, and I stopped wondering about Celia right then and there, and I began thinking instead of what he'd just said, and – jumping the gun – about what he was going to say. It all at once came to me clear as a bell. I could have read his speech even before it came out of his mouth.

'Thank you,' I said. 'I try to keep on my toes.'

'And you *do*. Which is why I'd like you to take Andy's place on any caper. Sort of supervise. Do you understand?'

'I sure do,' I said.

'Good. I like you, Frankie. I like you a lot. There's room for you at the top. You can be a big man, Frankie, a really big man.'

And that was it. I'd been tapped. I was made right that minute, and I knew it. This was no promise from a fat-assed Jobbo or a guy with the horns on him like Andy. This was straight from the horse's mouth, straight from Number One, straight from Mr Carfon who ran the whole damn shooting match. And what he said was there was room at the top. What he said was I could be a big man if I kept on being smart.

'I'm glad to hear that,' I said, and I had all I could do to keep from jumping right through the ceiling and starting to scream like a bird. But I kept calm because I'd bargained with this cookie before and always come out on the short end of the stick. From here on in, Mr Carfon wasn't never going to know what this boy was thinking or what this boy wanted. From here on in, it was cool, but the coolest.

'Say, I didn't think to ask,' Mr Carfon said, smiling. 'You didn't have any other plans for tomorrow night, did you?'

I could have said 'No' as quick as I could have said my own name. Celia was a great thing, don't misunderstand me. But there's an old proverb like, man, you should never lose your head over a piece of tail, and I wasn't going to lose what was coming my way over nobody – but *nobody!*

I made like I was thinking it over.

Then I said, 'No, Mr Carfon. No plans at all.'

6

So I didn't get to see Celia that next night, and I didn't get to see her for the next week either because Mr Carfon sent me to Pennsylvania to supervise the loading of some stuff going up to Canada. And then, when I got back I somehow didn't feel like calling Celia. I felt like calling May.

I suppose the head shrinkers could make something of that if they wanted to. I personally think that head shrinkers are only priests, and I stopped going to church when I was thirteen years old. The reason I stopped going to church was that I had just laid a girl named Josephine and when I went to confession I wanted to know something about it because this was the first time it happened to me and because my old man had never discussed anything like this with me, the way fathers in Scarsdale discuss these things with their sons who are on the goddamn junior varsity and who are making it with blonde, blue-eyed cheerleaders who live in twenty-room mansions.

I went to the priest because I figured he could set me straight, but he didn't set me straight at all. I kind of came out of that confession box feeling I done something very dirty and this was puzzling because it didn't feel dirty at all while I was doing it. So I automatically figured the priests had the wrong slant, and I stopped going to confession and then after a while I stopped going to church, too. I didn't miss it at all. It was good to sleep late on Sundays. I began eating meat on Fridays, too. There was only one danger to this. Like if you ordered a meat sandwich in a restaurant on Friday, people might think you was a Jew. I got enough troubles without people thinking I'm a Jew. So whenever I ordered a meat sandwich on Friday in a restaurant, I made sure the meat was *ham*. That way there wasn't no mistakes.

But what I'm driving at is that head shrinkers are only a new kind of priest. I heard through the grapevine that Mr Carfon had a head shrinker, but not for me, man. Can you imagine laying on a couch and telling somebody about how you used to wet your pants when you were four years old and your old man one time beat you with a broom because you spoiled a brand-new mattress and made it stink of piss? Just dig me doing that! It would be just the same as going to confession – except there's no Hail Marys afterwards.

So I called May instead of Celia, and I picked her up about seven thirty that night. She looked real crazy that night. She was wearing a pale blue sweater and a big bulky tweed skirt. It was still pretty mild in New York: sometimes New York gets like that, where it don't get real cold until maybe November or December, where you can walk around like it's still spring in September. She had only lipstick on her face, and her hair was brushed careless, but very careful naturally, so that she looked as if she'd been caught in a strong wind.

'I thought you'd forgotten me again,' she said, smiling and taking my arm.

'No. I was out of town for a while. You look real pretty tonight, May, you know that?'

'Why, thank you,' she said.

We walked downstairs to the stoop, and I waited for the surprise to register on her face. For a minute, it didn't take. So I walked over to the car and opened the door, and then those brown eyes of hers opened wide and she said, 'Is it yours?'

'Yeah. You like it?'

'Oh, it's *adorable*,' she said.

It was just a little Ford, not a new model, but with a new paint job. It had been waiting for me when I got back from Pennsylvania, together with a raise to a hundred a week. Mr Carfon said it was a sort of bonus for the fine job I'd done during the loading. I suspected the car was hot, but that didn't bother me none. If it was hot, I was sure it had been snatched somewhere on the West Coast, or maybe even in China for all I knew. Mr Carfon don't take chances, you see.

'Wasn't it terribly expensive?' May asked.

'It was a gift,' I said. 'My boss gave it to me.'

She climbed in, and I started the heap and then began driving uptown. After a little while, May asked, 'Who do you work for, Frankie?'

'A nice guy,' I said.

'What kind of work do you do?'

'All different kinds,' I said.

She paused a minute. 'Legal?'

'What?'

'Is what you do legal?'

'What difference does it make?'

'I don't know.'

I hesitated, and then I decided to play it straight, take it or leave it. 'It's illegal,' I said. 'Except sometimes. Mostly, it's illegal.'

'I see.'

'You want me to take you home now?'

'No. No, let's drive.'

'I'm kind of broke,' I said. 'I don't think we can – '

'That's all right. A drive'll be nice.'

I had about seven bucks in my pocket, and I knew I wouldn't be paid until Saturday. Mr Carfon was very strict about salary advances. He said he gave us a decent wage, and he expected it to last a week. If it didn't we could look for work elsewhere. He was very fair that way, Mr Carfon.

I drove uptown to the Grand Concourse, and then I kept going past Fordham Road, and then onto Mosholu Parkway, and then onto the Saw Mill. May was quiet for a long time.

At last she said, 'What illegal things do you do, Frankie?'

'May, I don't want to talk about it. Mr Carfon don't like us to talk about it with outsiders.'

'Am I an outsider?'

'Well . . . yes.'

'Suppose . . . suppose we were married, Frankie? Would I still be an outsider?'

'Married?' I digested this for a couple of minutes. One thing you had to say for May, she didn't believe in playing footsie. She got right to the point. 'I never gave it much thought,' I said.

79

'Think about it,' she answered.

'Well, a couple of the boys are married,' I said.

'Would you like to marry me, Frankie?'

'I thought it was the guy supposed to make the proposal,' I said. I was getting a little nervous. I mean, I don't mind aggressive dames, but you know marriage is a serious thing.

'I'm not proposing,' May said.

'Well, it sounds like it. Besides, my work is illegal. I don't think a wife – '

'You're young,' May said. 'You can change.'

'This is a good deal,' I told her. 'I don't think I'd *want* to change it.'

'We'll see,' she said. 'Why don't you park someplace, Frankie?'

'Okay,' I said. I drove along until we came to the next parkway exit. We hadn't yet hit the Merritt. We were still up around Rye someplace or maybe Port Chester. I turned off and then cruised around until I found a dark street. I yanked up the emergency brake and before I could even turn on the seat, May was in my arms.

'Kiss me, Frankie,' she said.

I kissed her. It was different from Celia. It was young and sweet and . . . I don't know . . . honest, I guess. It surprised me, her kiss. It surprised me because it was as if everything she was and everything she felt was in the sweetness of her mouth. I looked at her in surprise, and then I touched her lips with my fingers, and I said, 'Hey!'

'What?'

'Nothing. I liked that.'

'Then do it again.'

I kissed her again.

'I love you, Frankie,' she said. 'Do you know that?'

'No. I didn't – '

'For a long time,' she said, her voice very low. 'From when I first moved into the neighborhood. I used to watch you playing stickball on Sundays. You played first base.'

'Yes . . . '

'And do you remember the time you had a fight with Leo? When he broke your pusho. I watched you then, Frankie, and I was cheering you. I wanted to kill him myself, that mean – '

'I was just a little snotnose then,' I said.

'I know. But I loved you. When you first asked me out, I thought I'd die. I thought you'd never notice me. And then you seemed to like me – at least you kept asking me out. And I thought, maybe, maybe there's a chance.' She stopped. She caught her breath. '*Is* there a chance, Frankie?'

'I don't know,' I said. I really didn't.

'Do you think you could love me, Frankie?'

'We're talking too much,' I said.

She kissed me again, and I held her close to me, and there was the smell of soap in her hair, and the smell was very clean. And then she just snuggled up with her head buried in my shoulder and we listened to the radio music, and I could hear her gentle breathing, like a little kitten purring. It was nice. It was real nice.

I dropped her off about midnight. Her father was very strict, and he set limits about what time she should be home, especially on weekdays. Because it was so early, I looked around for some of the boys. I ran into Carrie first, down the poolroom. He had suckered some jerk into a game, and he was chalking them up like crazy, sinking one ball after the other. I waited until he finished his run, and then I took him aside.

'Where *is* everybody?' I asked.

'Up Weasel's pad,' he said.

'Doing what?'

'A poker session. You got some loot to spill?'

'A little. Is it a high-stakes game?'

'The usual. You going up there?'

'Maybe.'

'I'll see you later then. I'm heading there after I knock off this slob.'

'Gone,' I said.

I drifted out, not really feeling like poker, but wanting to think a little about May and about all the things she'd said. I don't go for this crap, you know, like is in all the women's magazines. I mean where the snotnosed kid next door who's all the time wearing pigtails and making horrible faces and who's got freckles all over her suddenly unloosens the pigtails and stops making faces, and all the freckles disappear except one very attractive one just above her cheekbone and all at once she's a dazzling dish and the hero falls in love with her. This is great for the ladies in Garden City, Long Island, who got nothing to do but shop Lord & Taylor's and then sit around munching French chocolates and thinking how nice it is that pigtailed, freckle-faced snotnoses can wind up with the heroes of the world. From my own experience, it seems to me like the ugly snotnoses of America wind up to be the ugly grownups of America, and the heroes go off marrying movie stars and then divorcing them a little while later.

All I'm trying to say is that May never *was* an ugly kid. Not that I can really remember what she actually looked like when she was wearing diapers. I never went over to her carriage and peeked in and said, 'Why, what a lovely little baby, you-are-for-me, doll!' But she never was ugly, that's for sure, and I was sort of surprised that suddenly I could begin thinking in love terms about her, after knowing her all these years. I know that's perfectly understandable to the ladies in Garden City, but to me it was confusing. I guess I always expected love to come up and hit me on the head with a ball bat. Who expects love to be wearing sneakers?

Well, I walked down to 116th Street and then up to Third Avenue and then I went into the tenement where Weasel lived. I climbed upstairs and knocked on his door twice. The door pulled back a little and Max's face showed and then split into a grin.

'Hey, Frankie,' he said. 'Hello, boy.'

He opened the door for me, and I went in. He's a short little guy, Max, who looks like the guy in all the garment-center jokes you hear. He never shaved very often, although he sure could have used it. I guess maybe he didn't like to shave, who does? He had a pot belly, and he wore his pants real low, so that you always thought his belly was gonna pop right out and spill over the floor. He had very tiny brown eyes. Actually, I never envied him because I tried to figure what it was like to be a kid named Max, and I don't believe it. There are actually no children in the world named Max. Max is only a name for grown men.

'You looking good, kid,' Max said. 'How's life treating you?'

'Fine. Where's the game?'

'In back.' He gestured with his head. 'You feeling lucky?'

'A little.'

'You loaded?'

'I got loot,' I lied.

'Can you spare a fiver?'

'What for, Max?'

'I was thinking a little mootah would hit the spot right about now.'

'You better lay off that stuff,' I told him.

'What for? Boy, there ain't nothing wrong with it.'

'That's what they all say.'

'The big stuff, sure. C and M and H, they're murder. But marijuana? Why, man, that never hurt a fly.'

'I can't spare a fiver, anyway,' I said. I paused. 'How come you need a fin for a little mootah? Who you snowing, Max?'

'Me? I ain't snowing nobody, Frankie.'

'You on hoss already? That it?'

'Hell, no,' Max said. 'You take me for an idiot?'

'Then what you need a fiver for? A fiver'll get you a cap of hoss. You don't need a fiver for a joint. You can get a joint for half a buck. Who you snowing, Max?'

'Okay, I was figuring on a *couple* of joints,' Max said. 'A stick don't get me high no more, Frankie. I need two, three.'

'That comes to a buck fifty in my country,' I told him. 'How come you need a fin?'

'All right, all right, I ain't playing with marijuana no more, all right? Man, when you busted enough joints, they don't give you that lift no more, you dig?'

'That's just what I been telling you. Man, you sound like you're hooked already.'

'Who, me? Hell, no. Just because I ain't hip to muggles no more? That don't mean nothing.'

'What *are* you on then?'

'You ever try opium, man?'

'I never tried nothing, and I ain't gonna start now.'

'Who's inviting you?' Max said, smiling. 'Come on, dad, loosen the five spot.'

'No,' I said.

'A deuce then. How about it?'

'For opium?'

'It's my poison, ain't it, man? I ain't asking advice. All I want is a deuce. Besides, opium's legal in China, didn't you know that?'

'That's why the Chinks are all frigged up,' I said. 'And this don't happen to be China. You better wise up, Max. You want to get anywhere in this outfit, you'll lay off the junk. Mr Carfon don't go for junkies. Hell, you seen what happened to Turk. He's back in Chicago because he was hooked. A few years, and you can forget he was ever a big man. He'll be laying in some alley with belly cramps. That's a real promotion, ain't it? Lay off it, Max. I'm telling you like a father.'

'You gonna lend me the deuce or nay?'

'No.'

'You broke? Is that it?'

'I'm loaded,' I said.

'Then slip me a deuce. Come on, Frankie, I ain't been straight since noon. I don't get a fix soon, I'll blow the top of my skull.'

'And you ain't hooked, huh?' I said sourly.

'Hooked, shmooked, the monkey don't know from words. You got a deuce or not? You're wasting my time.'

I fished into my wallet and laid a deuce on him. 'It's your funeral,' I said.

'What a friggin' way to die,' Max answered. 'Thanks, man. I'll pay you Saturday. I got to find me an engine, and then see a man about cooking up a pill.'

I left him to look for his opium pipe and the guy who'd sell him the gummy ball of crap to put in it. The game in the back room was a real quiet one. Weasel and Jobbo and Benny and a new guy I didn't know were sitting around the table in their shirt sleeves. None of the guys was heeled except Weasel. He had a .38 sticking out of a shoulder holster. He looked like as if he thought he was the star of *Detective Story*.

'Hi, boys,' I said, and all the boys gave me the nod but Weasel. Weasel looked like he was real busy with his cards. He held them in a tight fan, and he studied them like he'd just opened an Egyptian tomb.

'Draw?' I asked, and Weasel said, 'What the hell does it look like?'

'I was only asking,' I said.

'Well, that was a real bright question,' Weasel said. 'Every-body's holding five cards, and you ask if it's draw.'

'It could be Old Maid,' I said, grinning.

'Weasel's losing,' Jobbo explained.

'Gee, that's awful sad,' I said. 'Can I get in the game?'

'And share my dough another way? No, sir,' Weasel said.

'I'll be bringing fresh money into the game.'

'We got too many players already.'

'You only got four. We can still play draw with five players.'

'I don't want no debate,' Weasel said. 'The game's closed.'

'You mind if I watch?'

'So long as you shut up,' Weasel said.

'Yeah, but is it all right to breathe?'

Jobbo laughed, and then Benny began laughing, and even the new guy, a snotnose with a black pompadour, began laughing.

'Very funny,' Weasel said. 'We playing cards, or is this a sewing circle?'

I went over behind Jobbo's chair and took a look at his hand. He was holding a pair of queens, a lone ace, and two low-spot cards. Benny picked up the deck and said, 'Cards.'

The new kid said, 'One,' so I knew he was pulling for either a straight or a flush unless he was sitting with two pairs and openly advertising them by trying to triple one of them. Weasel had opened, and he called for three cards, so all he had was a pair, jacks or better. I saw Jobbo getting ready to discard three cards, including the lone ace, so I stuck my hand out and tapped the ace, and he looked up, and when I shook my head he kept the ace and discarded only the low-spots.

'Two,' he said.

Benny gave him the two cards, and then drew three for himself. I watched Jobbo as he squeezed out the cards he'd drawn. A five, and another ace. That gave him two pairs, queens and aces. He smiled and nodded. Weasel, the opener, said, 'Bet three.'

'Raise you two,' Jobbo said, throwing a fin into the center of the table.

'I'm out,' Benny said, folding his cards.

'Too steep for me,' the new kid said, so I knew he hadn't filled his hand.

Weasel looked at Jobbo, and then he looked at me, and then he put another deuce into the pot and said, 'I guess I have to call.'

'Two pair,' Jobbo said. 'Aces up.'

'It's your pot,' Weasel said sourly. 'Sonovabitching cards ain't been running right all night.'

Benny shoved the deck to the new kid and said, 'Your deal, Georgie.'

The kid took the deck, shuffling them like an expert, and then he dealt quickly. Weasel examined his cards and said, 'Pass.'

'Pass,' Jobbo said.

'I can open,' Benny said. He slipped a deuce to the center of the table, and everybody matched it.

'Cards,' George said.

'Two,' Weasel said, so I figured him for a low pair and an ace kicker. If he'd had a high pair or three of a kind, he'd probably have opened.

Jobbo was holding four hearts, and his fifth card was a five of clubs which paired up with the five of hearts. He was getting ready to discard the three hearts, saving the pair of fives. If he did that and didn't draw to the pair, Benny would certainly beat him with his jacks-or-better openers. And even Weasel could beat him if he caught another pair or the mate to that ace kicker he was holding. I shook my head, and Jobbo looked up at me. I tapped the five of clubs, telling him silently that he should discard that and take his chances on filling the heart flush.

'What the hell are you doing?' Weasel said.

I looked up. 'Huh?'

'You. What the hell are you doing?'

'Kibitzing,' I said.

'We don't need no kibitzers in this game,' Weasel said. 'How many friggin' guys am I playing against, anyway?'

'I was just – '

'You frigged up the last pot, and I didn't say nothing. Now I'm telling you to keep your goddamn mouth shut. Discard what you was gonna discard, Jobbo.'

'What for?' Jobbo said. 'This way is better.'

'Discard what you was gonna discard,' Weasel said tightly.

'What the hell!' Jobbo said. 'That don't make any sense.'

'You discard the right way, Jobbo,' I said to him. I turned to the kid dealing. 'One card.'

Weasel got up from the table, and then he put his palms down flat on the wooden top, leaning over so I couldn't miss seeing the butt of the .38 sticking out of the shoulder holster.

'You looking for trouble?' he said.

'No.'

'Okay, so don't – '

'But there's nothing wrong with kibitzing. Everybody kibitzes.'

'You're lousing up the game,' Weasel said. 'Let Jobbo play the way he wants to.'

'He don't have to follow my suggestions,' I said. 'Seems to me you're the one who's forcing him to play *your* way.'

'You'd better get the hell out of here,' Weasel said. 'You're stinking up the place.'

'The place stunk before I got here,' I said, and I balanced myself for what I knew was coming.

I saw Weasel's eyes narrow, and then one hand left the table and shot up for the .38 hanging in the shoulder holster. His hand tightened on the gun butt, but before he could pull the gun free I shoved out at his chest. He slammed back against the wall and then brought his hand up again, still trying for the gun, but I was already across the room.

As the gun came out, I clamped both hands on his wrist, and he yelled, 'You son of a bitch!' but I smashed the gun hand against the wall, just like I was swinging a bag, and I heard the crack when his knuckles hit the plaster, and then his fingers popped open, and the gun clattered to the floor. He dropped to his knees, trying to pick up the gun, and I stepped on his hand, bringing the heel of my shoe down hard, angry enough to break every goddamn bone in his body now. He pulled back his hand with a scream, and at the same time I brought back my foot and then let it go again, catching him right on the point of his jaw.

He flew over backwards, like a guy doing a fancy dive from a high board. I reached down and pulled him into my fist, and then I kept ramming my fist into his mouth, aiming for his teeth, wanting to knock every tooth out of his mouth. I held him up against the wall, just pounding at his mouth, feeling the teeth give, hitting him to make sure he knew I didn't take crap from nobody. Then I let him go, and he just fell back against the wall and then slid down to the floor.

I took out my handkerchief and wiped the blood off my knuckles.

'You better shovel him out of here,' I said. 'Manure decays fast.'

Some of the boys laughed – but not one of them made a move to pick up Weasel. I looked at him, and then I spit on the floor at his feet. Then I left the room and the friendly little poker game.

It was maybe because of the fight with Weasel that Mr Carfon decided to send me out of town again. He was very nice about the whole thing, but he said he didn't like 'internal' arguments, and he thought we both needed a little time to cool off. He said he had some business up Utica way, anyway, and he thought I'd be the best man to put things in order.

In any case, his decision accounted for a couple of things that maybe wouldn't have happened if I stuck around in New York. The first of these was the bust-up with Celia and this maybe accounted for a lot of things that were going to happen later on, but I don't want to get ahead of myself.

I got to explain what it was like with Celia. I mean, it was great. She was like an animal. I dig that with chicks. I like to see them smooth and polished, sleek as a piece of chrome, untouchable, with a class that says, 'Don't come near me; I can't be had.' And then you come near, and you touch, and the polish all drops away, the sleekness disappears, there's only a girl with mussed hair and bruised lips who's aching for you, a dame who all at once is an animal and who doesn't give a damn about anything but you. That sends me.

And that's the way it was with Celia. Like as if she was trying to find something with me. Like as if each time she screamed she was screaming out a prayer. Like that. With that blonde hair wild, and those green eyes staring up into my face, smoky, searching, and her lips parted on the edge of a scream or a moan, her eyes never leaving my face, hungering there, feeding there. That's what it was like.

So it was great. And at the same time, it was nothing. I mean, she knew things would make the Eiffel Tower melt. She knew tricks Houdini would have locked himself in trunks for. She used that crazy body of hers as if it was a machine answering any command she gave it, breast, tongue, mouth, eyes, every-thing, everything – and yet it was nothing. She knew it, and I knew it, only neither of us expected the other to say it.

And then, just before I left for Utica, Celia *did* say it.

I guess she'd had a drink or two before I got to the apartment. She opened the door, and she stood there in green pajamas and she cocked one eyebrow and said, 'Well, lover,' and from just the way she said those two words, I knew it was done between us almost before it had started, I knew this was the last time I'd see Celia. As it turned out, I was wrong. I was going to see Celia once more before the thing was really done, but that was under different circumstances.

'Come in,' she said, and she did a clumsy little curtsy and I went into the crumby flat and walked straight to the sofa and sat down.

'Remember the first time I was here?' I said. 'Boy, my leg – '

'Yes, I remember. You want a drink?'

'No.'

'I do,' she said. She poured from a bottle of whisky on the end table. 'Big-shot Andy Orelli,' she said, almost to herself. 'His wife likes Canadian Club. Do we drink Canadian Club? Look at what we drink.' She held out the bottle so I could see the label.

'There's worse,' I said.

'There's better,' she answered. She tilted the half-full water glass. 'Here's to crime,' she said. She giggled. 'It don't pay.'

'It pays,' I told her.

'Sure. Sure it does.' She nodded reflectively for a minute and then, out of a clear blue sky, she said, 'Go home, Frankie. There's nothing for you here any more.'

'What do you mean?'

'Nothing here. No pussy piece.' She giggled again. 'Nothing. You know something? There never *was* anything.'

I walked over to her. I put my hand on her shoulder and then ran it down her arm, and I let it rest on her hip, where the swell of her flesh pushed out at the green silk. 'There's plenty here,' I said.

'Nothing. Go home, Frankie.' She giggled. 'Yankee, go home. You are fondling a slut.' My hand dropped a little. She didn't move. She stood just where she was as my fingers closed on her. Then she shook her head. 'It won't work. No good, Frankie. Don't waste your time.'

I backed away and looked at her. 'What's the matter, all of a sudden?'

'All of a sudden? No. Not all of a sudden. A long time coming.' She shook her head again. 'It's no good, Frankie. I thought it might be. I thought maybe this would be it, you know? The shining white love everybody talks about, everybody writes about, but where is it I'd like to know? Where is it except in the movies?'

'Celia – '

'I thought maybe you.' She grinned. 'The pushover. Frankie the pushover. Wiggle an ankle, cock an eyebrow, and Frankie springs up like a switchblade knife. Young. Ripe. Delicious.' She paused. 'I got news. It isn't you. You're not the shining white love.' She paused again. 'It's almost ridiculous that I thought you were. It makes me feel like a very old woman.' She sat suddenly. 'Do you know what I am? The slut of the world. Everybody in the club has had me. I'm like the team letter. They

90

wear me on their sweaters. They haven't made varsity if they haven't made Celia. Men. Didn't any of them realize it was Celia doing all the making, Celia trying, trying, trying to find . . . what?' She gave a derisive little laugh. 'Even Celia doesn't know.'

'You've been drinking too much,' I said, and I took a step toward her.

'Yes. I've been drinking too much, and laughing too much, and oh, Jesus, crying too much, crying, crying.' She paused. 'Period. End. We get out.'

'What do you mean?'

'Andy and me. Out. Good-bye to Mr Carfon and his tight little club. Good-bye to Milt Hordzig and his fat wandering hands. Good-bye to Frankie Taglio and his switchblade, click! Click, click, *click!* You delicious bastard, get the hell out of here!'

I dropped down at her feet, and I grabbed her shoulders hard, and she said, 'No.' She said it the way I've never heard that word spoken in my life. She didn't mean yes, and she didn't mean maybe, and she didn't mean later. She meant no. *N-O*. Period. End.

'We're getting out,' she said tiredly. 'As soon as possible. As soon as I can talk Andy into it. We are folding our tents and sneaking away into the night. You know why? Because this stinks. All of it. Mr Carfon stinks, and his club stinks, and his money stinks, and *you* stink. And me. I'm the worst of all. Grab, grab, get it, get it all, put it all in Celia's hot little hands, but how does Celia come out of it all, how does dear Celia wind up? She winds up empty. Empty house, empty life. Nothing. Nothing. We give nothing. I want a baby.'

The last words surprised me because they didn't seem to have anything to do with what had come before them.

'Maybe there's a chance,' Celia went on. 'Maybe there's still a chance.'

'For what?'

'For happiness,' she said quickly, and all at once she didn't seem so drunk. She stared at me soberly and said, 'We deserve more than this, Frankie.'

'Speak for yourself,' I said. 'Just 'cause you're down in the dumps don't mean everybody – '

'Listen to me,' she said. 'You're not a bad kid. You can still – '

'Thanks.'

'If you were smart – '

'I *am* smart,' I said. 'Are you finished?'

Celia sighed. 'Yes. I'm finished.'

'And you still want me to go?'

'Yes.'

'Okay,' I said. 'So long.' I walked to the door. To tell you the truth, I felt a little relieved. I can't stand dames who suddenly come on like big thinkers.

'Frankie,' she said.

I turned. 'Yeah?'

'If you were smart – ' She studied my face a minute, and then she shook her head. 'Never mind.'

'That all?'

'That's all.'

'Then so long.'

The last thing she said before I walked out of the apartment was, 'It's a goddamn shame.'

She made me feel rotten.

I mean, first of all I was expecting *her*, you know, and not her mind. Minds are cheap. You can buy talk for the price of a glass of beer. And if she was going to run for president, why'd she greet me in them goddamn clinging pajamas and then act like a starved nympho about to enter a convent? Dames. Jesus! I'll never understand them as long as I live.

Also, what she *said* made me feel rotten.

I mean, what the hell, I never heard Mr Carfon say a word against being married or having kids. He probably liked the idea. It added to the front. And whose fault was it but her own if she felt like flopping in the hay with everybody in the outfit? (And *that* got me sore, too, if you want to know.)

But I guess the reason she really made me feel rotten was because all at once she made me feel alone.

I don't like to feel alone.

I like a lot of people around, you know?

She made me feel as if, I don't know. Like I'd be alone. Like . . . I don't know.

Anyway, I went to Utica feeling like hell, and Utica ain't exactly a town designed to cheer a guy up. Whenever I began thinking about what Celia had said, I began feeling sadder. And I was supposed to be there on business!

A lot of time I had for business. I was barely getting the feel of the joint when everything kind of happened at once. To begin with, I got a telephone call from Mr Carfon in New York telling me to look in on a guy named Osikras, and explaining what he wanted to know from this Osikras. It was around six o'clock when I got the call. I figured I'd drop in on Osikras that night, so I took a shower and I was dressing when a knock came on the hotel-room door. I went to open it.

'Hello,' May said.

She was standing in the doorway with a small suitcase in one hand. She was wearing a coat with a little fur collar, and she had a fur hat on her head that looked like something the Russian Cossacks used to wear. I was too surprised to say a word.

'It's me, all right,' she said, and she walked into the room and put her suitcase down on the floor, and then looked around the place and then nodded sort of, and then turned to me and said, 'Aren't you going to kiss me?'

'Well, sure, I – ' She came to me, and I kissed her, and she looked at me sort of sideways and then kissed me again and said, 'Mmmmmm.'

'Wh . . . what are you doing here?' I asked. 'In Utica.'

'I came to find you,' May said.

'How . . . how'd you know where . . . ?'

'I met Andy Orelli the other day. He told me where you were staying.'

'Oh,' I said. I thought for a minute. 'But . . . why'd you want to find me? I don't get it. Is something . . . ?'

May unbuttoned her coat, took it off, and threw it onto one of the chairs. She was wearing a blue suit under the coat. A white blouse showed under the blue jacket to the suit.

'We're going to get married,' May said.

'What? Who? *What?*'

'We,' she answered. 'You and me,' she answered. 'Married,' she answered.

'Hey, now – '

'Don't you love me?' she said, and she took off the suit jacket and threw it over the coat.

'Well, I don't know. I mean, Jesus, you don't believe in rushing a guy, do you?'

'Yes, I believe in rushing a guy,' she said, and cool as a cucumber, she began unbuttoning her blouse.

'May, listen – '

'I want to marry you,' she said flatly. She pulled the blouse out of her skirt and flipped it onto the chair. She was wearing a white bra, and she moved across the room toward me slowly, and then she undid the button on the side of her skirt. 'Don't you want to marry me?'

'I . . . I . . . don't know.'

Her hand paused on the zipper of her skirt. 'Think about it.'

'May,' I said. 'You better . . . you better put on your clothes. Come on, put on your clothes.'

'Why?' she asked, and she pulled down the zipper, and then shoved the skirt off her hips and stepped out of it when it hit the floor. She wasn't wearing a slip. She looked at me with cold, calculating eyes, as if all this was part of a plan, and she put her hands on her hips, and she sucked in a deep breath, and she stood with her legs just slightly apart, the panties cutting into the flesh of her thighs.

'Don't you want to marry me?' she said. 'Don't you *want* me, Frankie?'

Want her? I was scared of her. That's the plain honest goddamn truth. I was scared to death of her. She took a step closer to me. Her hands reached behind her to unclasp the bra, and suddenly she stopped, and she ran to me and threw herself into my arms, and began crying and saying, 'Oh, Frankie, I'm so ashamed, I'm so ashamed of myself,' and I said, 'Come on, May, don't cry,' and she said, 'I'll get dressed, I'm sorry. I'm so ashamed, don't look at me, I'll die if you look at me,' and I said, 'Come on, May, get ahold of yourself,' and all the while she was in my arms, and her skin was warm under my fingers and

suddenly I pulled her close to me, and I grabbed her hair and
yanked her head back and she came up against me, and I kissed
her harder than I've ever kissed any girl in my entire life, and
then my hands were all over her because she was the softest,
sweetest thing I'd ever held, her mouth was like honey, honey.

'I love you,' she said.

'Yes.'

'I love you, I love you.'

'May, May baby . . .'

'Say it.'

'May, baby . . .'

'Frankie, say it to me. Frankie, say it!'

'I love you!' I said, and it was almost a moan of some kind.
'Oh, May, I love you. I love you, May. I love you. I love you.
I love you. I love you. I love you.'

We got married by a magistrate in Utica as soon as we'd got
the wedding license and the blood test which New York State
requires. I called Mr Carfon to tell him about it, but he wasn't
in. Milt Hordzig took the message and said he would let Mr
Carfon know. He also told me not to forget the business I had
with the Greek. By the Greek, he meant Osikras, which is what
he was.

I guess maybe I was hoping Mr Carfon would call back to tell
me how pleased he was. Actually, I didn't know whether he'd be
pleased or not, though I couldn't see any reason for him to ob-
ject. Lots of guys in the organization were married.

On Saturday morning, just as we were getting out of bed, a
wire came. It was addressed to Mr and Mrs Frank Taglio. It
said: CONGRATULATIONS AND ALL GOOD WISHES. FRED
CARFON.

About a half-hour after that, two dozen red roses came from
Mr Carfon. They were addressed to May, and there was a small
card inside and on the card it said, in Mr Carfon's own hand-
writing, 'For the new bride who, I'm sure, is lovely.'

'You see?' I said. 'Now is he such a bad guy?'

'It was very considerate of him,' she said.

'Come here,' I told her.

We had a wonderful time all the while we were in Utica. Of course, I was also there on business, and that cut into our time a lot, but May understood. Or at least I thought she did.

My business was with this guy named Ralph Osikras, mostly. What he done, this Greek, he disposed of hot stuff that Mr Carfon sent up to him. He was a skinny guy who wore black all the time, like an undertaker. His eyes were dark brown, and his brows and hair were black. He had a lot of blackheads all over his face, the dirty Greek. He gave you the impression of some kind of vulture when you looked at him.

The rumble had got to him about my arriving, of course, and the first time I met him he was very cordial. His front was a drugstore, and he took me into the back room and shooed out his pharmacist and then he sat me down and broke out some vintage wine. One thing I learned since working for Mr Carfon was how to tell good stuff from junk. When I saw that jug of wine, I already began thinking this Greek was a guy with luxury taste.

'So,' he said. 'So what's on Mr Carfon's mind, hah?'

'Mr Carfon wants me to check into the operation here,' I said.

'There's something wrong with the operation?'

'We don't know yet, Greek. That's why I'm here.'

'You're a new man, hah?'

'Yeah. What of it?'

'No, I just wonder, that's all. I mean, we have checks before, but always from one of the Utica boys. You come all the way from New York, so I wonder.'

'Yeah, well don't wonder so much. Mr Carfon wanted it done *right* this time, that's all.' I paused. 'Maybe Mr Carfon don't trust the usual Utica boys.'

'What's to trust?' Osikras said. 'You send me the stuff, I fence it. What's to trust?'

'You got books, Greek?'

'Books? Hey, you crazy? Books! You think maybe I'm in the wholesale dress business or something?'

'You better start keeping them, Greek. Right this minute.'

'What about the police?'

'Never mind the police. We been keeping our own books for a little while now, Greek, and we been wondering about the sudden drop in figures.'

'Money not so loose any more,' Osikras said. 'Times are bad.'

'That's what I'm here to check on.'

'So check.' He shrugged. 'I'm clean. Mr Carfon knows that. He knows I'm clean.'

'We'll see.'

'This stuff he sends me, this not diamonds, you know. It's hard to peddle hot furs, hot cars. A diamond, you chop it up, it's not recognize. You can't do that with this other stuff. Money's tight.'

'We don't expect a fortune, we only expect fair prices.'

'The money's been fair,' Osikras said. 'It's just tight, that's all. My young friend, you can't squeeze blood from a stone.'

'No,' I said, 'but you can sure as hell squeeze it from a head,' and the Greek looked at me very peculiarly.

I did a lot of nosing around. I traced the operation from the warehouse where the hot stuff was stashed, down to the receiver who kept contact with our New York man, right up the line to the big buyers who later peddled the stuff themselves for whatever it would bring. I checked all the figures. I checked the receiving dates and the disposal dates, and I began checking the books Osikras started to keep. I wired New York for the figures we had, and I checked the Greek's new figures against our old ones, and all of a sudden it seemed money wasn't so tight any more, all of a sudden there was a big increase in prices being paid, everything got real loose, a miracle must have suddenly happened in Utica. From the buyers, I found out what prices were being paid – and what prices had been for the past six months. Maybe Osikras thought he was dealing with the local hicks again, but this was New York on the wire, man, that long distance phone was ringing, man, this was the real stuff.

I went to him the last week May and me was in Utica. I showed him the figures the buyers had given me, and I showed him how they tallied against what we'd been raking in from this part of our operation in Utica. I also showed him how suddenly the miracle had come to pass and prices were now back to what they'd been in those good old free-swinging, loose-moneyed days, how all of a sudden prices jumped back up again when I appeared on the scene.

'What's the story, Greek?' I said.

'What you mean, what's the story? To begin with, those bastards lying. No matter what they say, they *were* paying lower prices a few months back. That's the truth.'

'Yeah? And how about now? All the prices jumping back up again?'

'I don't control the market,' Osikras said. 'I only sell for what I can get, and I send New York the proper amount. I'm to blame because those bastards lying?'

'Only one person lying, Greek. That's you.'

'Me? Me?'

'What's Mr Carfon paying you, Greek?'

'Ten per cent of what I get. Whatever I sell for, my take is ten per cent.'

'Ain't that enough for you?'

'I don't know what you mean.'

'I will write it on the wall for you, Greek. In the month of May, you pocketed an extra grand. In June, you put away three grand. In July, fifteen hundred. In August – a bad month, huh, Greek? – four hundred and fifty bucks. In September, twenty-two fifty. Last month – '

'No, you mistaken,' Osikras said.

'No, *you're* mistaken,' I told him. 'You're mistaken if you think you're going to fool around with us. You're taking money out of Mr Carfon's pocket, Greek, and that means you are also taking money out of my pocket.'

'No,' Osikras said. 'No, I am not.'

'Figures don't lie, Greek. Only Greeks do.' I took out the .45.

'Wh – what you going to do?' Osikras said, backing away from me.

'Mr Carfon wants you to know you ain't indispensable, Greek. He wants you to know the next time you step out of line, the next time there's even a goddamn penny short in the reckoning, I'll use the *other* end of this gun on you.'

'The other end? What you . . . what you . . . ' He was backing up against the wall. He was beginning to shake, a skinny stinking Greek vulture with all his feathers shaking.

'The other end, Greek. The end with the hole. For now, I use the butt. I use the butt to teach you a lesson, you understand? No more dipping in the kitty, Greek. This is the last warning. You understand, Greek? We want all the dough you pull in, less your ten per cent. No padding that percentage, Greek, you understand?'

I brought the .45 up, and then I slashed the butt down across his face, ripping open his cheek.

'No,' he said. 'Please, no, please, I – '

'You understand, Greek?' I said, and then I hit him again. And then I kept slashing the gun across his face, hitting him again and again and again, and finally leaving him on the floor to think over what I'd said.

I think he understood. I think, at last, he understood.

7

When we got back to New York, I wanted to take May around to meet Mr Carfon, but she said no. Actually, I couldn't understand her attitude. Mr Carfon had been real pleased with the work I done in Utica and had laid a little extra cash on me, which was just what we needed at the time. I mean, when you're first married you got to furnish an apartment and all. Mr Carfon understood that. As a matter of fact, he seemed pretty pleased that I'd taken the plunge. He kept calling me 'the respectable married man.' I guess that idea of respectability appealed to him, even though he ain't a bum. Nobody could ever think Mr Carfon was a bum, not with that pad he's got.

The pad we had, May and me, was the one I'd been living in all along. I didn't like the idea of moving in with my mother, but we couldn't find an apartment just like that, so we had to do it. A guy feels eerie messing around with a girl, even though she's his wife, when his own mother is in the next room. Anyway, that's the way *I* felt. So May and me went out looking for an apartment every day. That's how I spent most of my time after I got back from Utica. Until the jewelry store job came up. *That* goddamned job, I needed it like a hole in the head.

But it came up, and it broke the nice pattern of things being quiet, of going places during the day with May, having lunch with her, looking for the apartment, doing things like that. I didn't mind being married at all, actually. It was kind of nice. It changed the minute the jewelry store job came up.

The jewelry store was on Fifth Avenue. I know right away that when Fifth Avenue is mentioned everybody falls into the trap of thinking it's *Fifth Avenue*, Fifth Avenue. Everybody right away thinks of Lord & Taylor, and Tiffany's, and the Doubleday Book Shop, and Saks because this is what Fifth

Avenue means to most New Yorkers and even to out-of-towners. I guess *especially* out-of-towners.

Well, Fifth Avenue is a long street. It starts down in the Village and it goes up past the department stores around Thirty-fourth Street and then the buildings where all the publishing brains hang out, and the fancy jewelry shops, and past Fifty-seventh Street where all the art galleries are, and then it runs alongside the park all the way up to 110th Street, and then Fifth Avenue changes and becomes Spanish Harlem.

The change is a very quick one. It don't look too bad around Ninety-seventh, and it don't look too bad either around 105th, and then you're on 110th and whammo! there's Harlem. It's the same wide street, but all of a sudden it's a poor street. All of a sudden, there's tenements and stores with Spanish signs, and there's kids running in the streets, and there's a housing project up around 112th, 113th, and it's Harlem. That's the only way to say it. It's Harlem. And Harlem is a lot farther from Saks Fifth Avenue than the lousy fifty blocks or so that separate them.

This jewelry store we were going to knock over was in Harlem. The guy who ran it was a Puerto Rican who didn't make very much money, but we didn't go for this Robin Hood bit of stealing from the rich. The shop figured to be a pushover. Mr Carfon thought two guys could handle it, and maybe we would realize a couple of grand on the job and that was it. But the risk was pretty small, and the job would be a real quickie, so it was worth taking the gamble for the few grand.

Weasel and me were the two guys who were going to knock over the shop.

'I don't think this is such a good idea,' I said to Mr Carfon.

'Why not?'

'Weasel and me ain't exactly the best of friends,' I said.

'The shop is wired,' Mr Carfon said. 'I need Weasel for the alarm.'

'Well, sure, but – '

'Would you rather I sent someone else in your place?'

'I ain't trying to chicken out, Mr Carfon. It's just – '

'I've already spoken to Weasel,' Mr Carfon said. 'He's rather

101

ashamed of the way he behaved that night of the card game. He's admitted that he was needling you, and that he probably deserved what he got.'

'Well . . .'

'Of course, I can send someone in your place. There's this new kid, Georgie. I think he's going to be valuable, and he can use experience. Shall I send him?'

'No, Mr Carfon,' I said. 'I'll go.'

May started up with me that night when I was getting ready to leave.

First she wanted to know where I was going.

'On some business,' I told her.

Then she wanted to know what kind of business.

'Don't worry your pretty little head about it,' I said.

'I do worry.'

'Well, don't. This is going to be a pushover.'

'Is it a holdup?' she asked.

'No.'

'A burglary?'

'Come on, May. What difference does it make?'

'Are you going to carry a gun?'

'Yes.'

'Will you use it?'

'Not unless I have to.'

'Will you have to?'

'How the hell do I know? Look, don't worry about it. I can take care of myself.'

'Frankie?'

'What?'

'Is it worth it? Is what you have to do worth the money you bring home?'

'Yes,' I said. 'It's worth it.'

'You could . . . you could get lots of jobs,' she said. 'You're smart. You'd do a good job no matter who hired you.'

'Doing what?' I said. 'Running an elevator? Delivering groceries? What did you have in mind?'

'You don't have to deliver groceries,' May said. 'A lot of businesses have training programs.'

'Starting at what? Sixty-five bucks a week?'

'We could get along on sixty-five a week. I could take a job, too.'

'My wife don't work,' I said.

'Frankie – '

'I'm making a hundred and a quarter a week now, and this is just the beginning. How'm I supposed to get along on sixty-five?'

'You'd be doing honest work,' May said.

'What's so honest about big business? They steal from the customers, and they steal from the government when it comes tax time. I don't see any difference between big business and what I'm doing.'

'Don't you ever think ahead, Frankie?'

'I always think ahead. You know what Andy Orelli pulls down? Four bills a week. That's more than twenty grand a year! And I'll bet Milt Hordzig is already in the forty-, fifty-thousand-dollar bracket.'

'That's not what I meant, Frankie.'

'No? What did you mean?'

'I mean . . . don't you ever think of what you want?' She paused. 'Out of life?'

'I want all I can get,' I said flatly.

'Don't you want a home and – '

'How'm I gonna get a home on sixty-five a week? Sure I want a home. Don't you think I want to live in New Rochelle in a nice little house with a sprinkler going on the front lawn? Don't you think I want a new car in the garage, and a dishwasher, and nice clothes for you? I want all those things, May. I want them so bad, I can taste them! And this is the way to get them. This is the only goddamn way.'

'It isn't the only way, Frankie.'

'No? You think my old man was a lawyer who was going to take me into the firm? You think I got sent to medical school? You think I had my own little car when I was seventeen? You think I ever knew anything but the streets of Harlem? Don't be stupid, May. For guys like me, there ain't no gray flannel suits. I do it my way, or I don't make it at all. I've got to get what I want and need. And I need all I can get.'

'And what about your children? How will they feel when they know their father is a – '

I turned on her quickly. 'You're not . . . ?'

'Not what?'

'You're not . . . you know . . . we're not having a baby, or anything?'

'No.'

'Okay.'

'But when we *do* have – '

'We'll worry about it then,' I said. 'For now, let's drop it.'

'No, let's not drop it. Let's talk about it.'

'I don't want to.'

'I *do*, Frankie, and – '

'It'll have to wait. It's midnight, and I'm supposed to meet Weasel downstairs.' I went over to her and kissed her. 'Come on, grin.'

'Be careful,' she said, but she didn't smile.

'I will.'

In the car, Weasel said, 'We got a job to do, Frankie. In case you got any ideas I hold hard feelings, I don't.'

'I'm glad to hear that,' I said.

'Sure, it's all water under the bridge. I just want you to know, I don't hold any hard feelings. Okay?'

'Fine,' I said, and we drove to knock over the jewelry store.

The store was on Fifth Avenue, in the middle of the block. The back of the store opened on a little courtyard which you could reach by going behind the apartment house which was on the corner of the side street. I don't know if you've ever been underneath or behind a tenement. The way it works is there are steps leading down from the sidewalk to a little alley where the super puts the garbage cans. There's like a covered section under the front stoop, and then this alley that runs back on the side of the tenement. There's always a stink under the stoop and in the alley. There's a chain hanging from two iron posts on either side of the steps. The chain don't stop nobody from going down. Most of the time, the chain is just used like a swing by the kids. Every tenement has this chain and the steps and the alley, and they come out into a big common back yard which is divided with fences, but the fences are easy to climb over.

We didn't go down the steps of the corner tenement because, even at twelve thirty, there was some teen-age kids hanging around on the front stoop, talking Spanish. I was hoping maybe they belonged to one of the hot-shot street gangs. I would have liked to start up with the strangers in their territory, just so we could have mopped up the street with them. But they didn't say nothing or do nothing. They just hung around mushing it up with the girls with them.

We kept walking up the side street until we came to a tenement where nobody was on the stoop. We went over the chain and down the steps, and then to the alley. The clotheslines were flapping over our heads. They usually run from the kitchen windows to a wooden pole alongside the fence that separates one building's back yard from the next. There was a pretty strong wind that night, and the clothes were flapping like bastards. It was eerie. We went down the alley quick, and then jumped up to the stone wall where there was a little ledge that the fence was set in. Then we climbed the fence, and I kept hoping there wouldn't be no dogs in any of the back yards. I got a fear of dogs. This fear comes from once I was going to church on a Sunday morning and this little mutt comes in my way and just stands there on the sidewalk and bares his teeth and makes that sound in his throat like he's getting ready to put away a leg of lamb. 'Get out of my way,' I said to him, but he kept growling.

So I started to walk around him, and that was when he bit me. I don't mean he just took a nip and then ran away. I mean he sank his teeth in and started to gnaw away and the way I finally got him off was to punch him on his nose hard with my closed fist. That opened his jaws, and then I kicked him as hard as I ever kicked anybody or anything in my life, and I think maybe I killed the little bastard, I ran away from him bawling, with my pants all torn and my leg bleeding and, naturally, there was a visit to the clinic, always the goddamn clinic. They had to give me a rabies shot, and if you never had one, don't. That's why I got a fear of dogs. Dogs to me mean only one thing – pain. When the Russians shot that pooch up in the sky – even though I naturally hate the Russians and the Communists, who don't? – I was tickled to death. I kept hoping they would send up a big doghouse with all the dogs in the world in it. Then the comets could blast them all to pieces, good-bye Charlie.

So, as we climbed those fences between the yards, I kept wishing there was no hounds around. A hound would have fouled up that job as sure as a cop would have. Thank God, no hounds appeared. We got to the back of the jewelry store and Weasel sniffed around a while before he found the alarm box, and then he went to work on the wires and *poof*, he had the thing knocked off in about three seconds. We went to work on the back door then which was like a fire door, heavily covered with metal. But if you know how to bust open a lock, it don't matter if a door is made of concrete and steel forty feet thick – and we knew how to bust the lock. Which we done. Then we went into the store and closed the door, and started picking up whatever was around.

There was a safe in back, but this wasn't a safe job. We didn't have time to get the really priceless gems – ha! in a lousy two-bit jewelry shop! – that was in the safe. We just cleaned out all the cases, taking the watches and the pen-and-pencil sets and the bracelets and necklaces and whatever there was around. We put all the stuff in a satchel Weasel had. It was pretty simple.

We were getting ready to leave when we saw the cop.

He was just a regular uniformed cop who was making his rounds, trying all the front doors of the shops. It always strikes me ridiculous that the cops try the front doors. Do they really think a crook'll go in that way and then leave the door open? I think it just gives them something to do on the graveyard shift. Anyway, here came this cop trying all the doors. Naturally, Weasel and I ducked behind the counter. The cop came up to the door and pushed on it, and then he stuck his hands alongside his head and peeked through the window, past the grillwork on it.

He was moving away from the door when something hit me on the back of the head and I went crashing into the glass display case.

8

If you never been inside a police station, don't go, because it ain't much kicks. Don't, in fact, ever get involved with the Law, not even on a speeding ticket. Cops are absolutely the worst possible people in the world, especially if you are poor. This is the truth. If a rich man kills somebody, the cops come to his house and are usually a little apologetic for busting in at this time of night, Mr Gotrocks, but this is our duty, we are sure you understand. If you're poor, and you spit on the sidewalk, a cop will bust your head just as soon as look at you.

My head didn't need no busting that night. Weasel done a fine job of busting my head. He must have hit me with all the power of his arm behind the gun. I felt an explosion at the back of my head, and then I pitched forward and I must have crashed right through the glass top of the case because my hands and my face were all cut up when I came to. Where I came to was in the Detective Squad Room of the precinct house.

I'm exactly six feet tall, not an inch shorter and not an inch taller, but every bull in that squad room towered over me. I think sometimes they hire bulls only if they are big. They certainly can't hire them for brains. There is nothing a bull likes better than to sink his claws into what he thinks is a hood. Bulls are like generals. Generals ain't no good if there's no war on. So bulls are worthless if there ain't no crooks. When they get a hood in the station house, they figure this is a good time to prove we're worth something, this is a good time to show crime don't pay, we better take advantage of this skirmish because Christ knows when we get a chance again.

I came to because somebody threw water in my face. I jumped up out of the chair, and a big beefy paw clamped down on my shoulder and shoved me back again, and then of course I realized I was surrounded by bulls.

'Well, well,' one of the bulls said. Him I didn't like right off. He was Irish. I knew that the minute he opened his mouth. He didn't have a brogue or nothing, but I can tell an Irishman right away.

'What's your name?' another bull said.

'Frankie Taglio,' I told him. 'I want to make a phone call.'

'Relax, Frankie,' the Irish bull said. 'You got all the time in the world to make your phone call. You got a record, Frankie?'

'No.'

'You never been in trouble before?'

'Never.'

'This is the first time you been on a burglary?'

'Who says I burgled anything?' I asked.

'Maybe he didn't,' the Irish bull said. 'Fellers, maybe the owner of the store just forgot he was there and locked him in when he went home. Is that right, Frankie?'

'Maybe.'

He slapped me across the mouth, and the other bulls didn't do nothing to stop him.

'I suppose the owner of the store cut his own alarm system, huh, Frankie?'

'I don't know nothing about it,' I said, and he slapped me again, and I said, 'Keep your friggin' mitts off me,' and he slapped me again. I jumped out of the chair and went for him, and this time he hit me in the gut, doubling me over, and then punched me in the mouth, knocking me back in the chair.

'Lay off, Pete,' one of the other bulls said.

'What for?' Pete the Irish bastard said. 'He cut himself on the display case, didn't he? We didn't lay a hand on him.'

'We ain't getting anything else out of him, anyway,' the second bull said.

'No? Who was on the job with you, Frankie?'

'What job?'

'Who ran away with the loot?'

'I don't know what you're talking about,' I said.

Pete the Irish bastard got ready to hit me again, but the

108

second bull said, 'Lay off,' and so he laid off. I guess he was tired, or maybe it was time for his coffee break.

Instead of hitting me, they booked me and then took me down to the detention cells on the ground floor. The next morning, a police van came for me and they took me to the lineup at Headquarters downtown on Centre Street. What they do there, they put you on this stage, and bulls from all over the city are there to look you over while the Chief of Detectives asks you questions. I knew enough not to say anything. Everything he asked me, I just said I didn't know what he was talking about. By this time, they'd already checked and knew I didn't have no record. So I figured I'd be all right as soon as I could get to a phone and call Mr Carfon.

I called him right after the lineup. He said he would have a lawyer there immediately, and I was not to go for my arraignment until the lawyer showed up. He asked me if I had admitted anything, and I said no, and he said good, don't. I barely managed to get in he should have somebody call May to tell her what happened. Then he hung up.

As it turned out, May already knew what happened, that's how fast the word goes in Harlem. But of course they weren't letting me have no visitors right then, what the hell I hadn't even been arraigned yet. So the first guy I saw was the lawyer Mr Carfon sent down.

His name was David Lipschitz – a name which always used to break me up whenever I heard it as a kid, but which didn't break me up now because he was there to help me. He was a little guy who walked with little jerky movements like a bird. He moved his hands like a bird, and his head like a bird, and he kept pursing his lips. He must have been about sixty years old, but he didn't look a day over ninety. His eyes were very shrewd, though. Well, maybe that's a crock. Since that time, I met guys who I thought had shrewd eyes, and they turned out to be close to morons who could hardly speak two straight words together without babbling. And I met guys who had stupid-looking eyes, sleepy eyes, dopey eyes, and they turned out to be as sharp as a Caddy's fins. So I don't really believe you can tell nothing from the eyes. Eyes is just an accident of the face and got nothing to do with what's inside the head. But Lipschitz had eyes that looked shrewd, and it turned out he *was* pretty shrewd, too.

'You're in trouble, boy,' he told me – as if I didn't know.

'What'd they book me for?' I said. 'Grand larceny?'

'No, not grand larceny. They may have had a choice, true. In your case, grand larceny could have applied. Stealing property of the value of more than five hundred dollars, in any manner whatever, in the nighttime. But they've got a stronger charge.'

'What? Breaking and entering?'

'Unlawfully entering a building, do you mean?' Lipschitz said.

'I don't know,' I told him.

'That's only a misdemeanor,' he said. 'Section 405 of the Penal Law. "A person who, under circumstances or in a manner not amounting to a burglary, enters a building or any part thereof, with intent to commit a crime." No, they haven't got you on anything as simple as that. No misdemeanor, young man.'

'What's the difference between a misdemeanor and a felony?' I asked. It may sound funny that I didn't know, but who the hell ever thinks of such things?

'A felony is a crime which is punishable by death or imprisonment in a state prison. Any other crime is a misdemeanor. Most misdemeanors are not very serious. Speeding, for example, is a misdemeanor. So is spitting in the subway. *You* are charged with a felony.'

'What's the charge?'

'Third-degree burglary.'

'Is that bad?'

'Well, it could have been a lot worse. Let me explain it to you.'

'Okay,' I said. 'Explain it.'

'There are three types of burglary. First degree, second degree and third degree. The maximum penalties for each respectively are thirty years, fifteen years and ten years. Do you understand so far?'

'Yes,' I said.

110

'All right. Burglary in the first degree is defined as breaking and entering, in the nighttime, the dwelling house of another, in which there is at the time a human being. You can be armed with a dangerous weapon or you can arm yourself therein with such a weapon, or you can be assisted by a confederate actually present.'

'That don't sound so good,' I said.

'You were armed with a dangerous weapon,' Lipschitz agreed, 'and they can assume you were assisted by a confederate. But that still doesn't amount to first-degree burglary because there was no other person in the store. *Second*-degree burglary also has in its definition the presence of another human being. There was not, am I right, another person in that store when you entered it?'

'No. Nobody was in it.'

'That's why the charge is third-degree burglary. You broke into or entered a building, or a room, or any part of a building with intent to commit a crime – '

'How the hell do they know what my intentions were?'

'They don't have to. The second part of Section 404 of the Penal Law states, "or, being in any building, commits a crime therein and breaks out of the same." '

'Yeah, well I didn't break out. I was carried out.'

'Unfortunately,' Lipschitz said.

'So where do we stand?'

'You're charged with third-degree burglary. The fact remains, you see, that a burglary *was* committed, property *was* removed from that store. That's why you weren't charged simply with unlawful entry. The court must assume the store was entered with burglary in mind, and that your accomplice – if such he was – made off with the stolen property. We're lucky no one was in the store. In The People *vs* Hickey, 1923, it was upheld that an essential ingredient of the crime of burglary, first degree, is that breaking and entry must be in the nighttime, into the dwelling of another, *in which there is at the time a human being*. We're lucky.'

'Yeah, but we're also unlucky.'

'That's true. Please don't forget that you were carrying a

weapon and that you do not have a permit for that weapon. Do you?'

'No.'

'That's an offense,' Lipschitz said. 'A misdemeanor.'

'I thought it was a felony.'

'Only if you've previously been convicted of a crime. You do not have, I understand, a prior criminal record.'

'No, I don't. How much can I get for the gun rap?'

'The Penal Law sets no sentence for this particular misdemeanor.'

'So what do I get?'

'The court will set its own sentence for the gun violation. I doubt if it will exceed more than a year in a county workhouse. It could be ninety days, or sixty days or – in a first offense, such as this – you may receive a suspended sentence, with or without probation.'

'The real thing to worry about, then, is the burglary, right?'

'Yes. You can get a maximum of ten years for that. *If* we admit that you were a party to the burglary. But I believe we can get around that.'

'How?'

'By maintaining that you were in that store trying to *prevent* a burglary!'

'*Prevent* one? Who the hell would –'

'Yes. You heard noises in the store. You went in and tried to stop the burglar. He hit you. The police arrested you while the real burglar got away.'

'I see.'

'This is, of course, in direct contradiction to the facts. Weasel has already told us how you tripped and fell into one of the display cases just as a policeman –'

'What! Why, that two-bit phony! He slugged me from behind! He was the one responsible for –'

'Shhhhh, shhhhh,' Lipschitz said.

I lowered my voice. 'Is that what he told Mr Carfon? That I tripped and fell?'

'Yes.'

'That lying son of a bitch! When I get out of here – '

'Let's get you out first, Frankie.'

'All right,' I said, still burning. 'We say I was trying to stop a burglary, right? What about the gun?'

'We will admit that you were carrying the gun without a permit. This is not an uncommon occurrence in low-income neighborhoods.'

'And for that I'll get ninety days, huh?'

'You may get as much as a year, but I doubt it. My guess is ninety days.'

'That still sounds lousy,' I said. 'What do we do now?'

'We go across the street to the Criminal Courts Building for arraignment. The arraignment is simply a hearing of the charges against you. It will be determined then whether or not the charges will be dismissed or prosecuted. You can take my word for it that the charges against you will be prosecuted.'

'Will I go to jail?'

'To await trial after the arraignment? No, I don't imagine so. Bail will undoubtedly be set for you.'

'And then what?'

'Then your case will eventually come to trial.' He paused. 'Of course, we may get the right judge.'

'What do you mean, the right judge?'

'Mr Carfon knows a great many people, Frankie. Justice may be blind, but she instinctively knows where to reach for the long green.'

'Ain't that dangerous?'

'Not with the right judge, it isn't.'

'You think Mr Carfon knows the right judge?'

'I can assure you that he does indeed.'

'And he'll go to bat for me?'

'He sent me, did he not? And he's ready to pay your bail. But knowing the right judge, and wanting the right judge, and even being willing to pay the right judge, doesn't necessarily mean we'll get him. Court calendars – '

'I understand, I understand,' I said.

'Let's get the hearing over with,' Lipschitz said. 'Please don't say anything now which will contradict any later statement you will make at the trial. You were in that store to prevent a burglary, remember that.'

'I'll remember it,' I said.

They took us across the street, and I got arraigned. The charge was third-degree burglary. A bail was set and a bondsman Mr Carfon sent down paid it. I went home and waited for the trial, hoping we'd get the right judge.

Well, we got the right judge.

I got sixty days in the workhouse on Riker's Island.

9

There is nothing like a liberal education.

In those sixty days, I got a liberal education. I also missed Christmas and New Year's at home. We got turkey on Christmas Day. Also May came to visit. Where you get the ferry for Riker's Island is off Bruckner Boulevard in the Bronx. You go down 138th Street and the ferry is over on 135th or 136th, I can't say exactly because it's right on the river and who looks at the signs? There are big rats there on the wharf. I swear to God, they are the biggest rats I ever saw in my life, they look like tomcats. I lived in a lot of Harlem apartments, and they got their share of rats and mice and every other kind of crawling thing, but the rats in Harlem looked like cockroaches – of which there is also plenty in Harlem – compared to the rats on the dock where the ferry goes to Riker's. The same ferry also goes to North Brother Island which is where they keep the junkies. May told me she got talking with the mother of a young kid who is on North Brother and how what a pity it was the kid was hooked and all.

It seems the kid started when he was eleven years old and that, man, is some kind of a record, I guess. He'd been on the junk for six years before his old lady tipped to the fact that maybe something was rotten in Denmark – that is what I call a remarkable and observant old lady. I guess she tipped because her son was floating up around the ceiling of the room one day, full of H, and she figured my it is strange how Sonny is floating around up there near the ceiling. I think I will ask him what is wrong. So she finally learned her son had been shooting poison in his body since he was practically old enough to walk, a great mother, that old lady. And she blew the whistle on him, and now he was going the cure on North Brother.

From what I could see on Riker's, there was an awful lot of junkies who managed to get out of their teens without their mothers blowing the whistle, and who were still shooting themselves full of poison. I never knew there were so many junkies in all the world. I also never knew there were so many drunks. Or vagrants. Or fairies. Or thieves of every kind you want to name, guys who done things so disgusting I don't even want to talk about it. To tell the truth, it was an entirely disgusting experience being shut up on Riker's Island for sixty days with this crawling bunch of humans. It taught me a lesson, all right. When I got out of there in January, I had it all straight. I knew exactly what was right and what was wrong.

It was wrong to get caught.

I made up my mind that I was never gonna get caught again.

I also made up my mind that I was gonna kill Weasel as soon as I got the chance.

I didn't tell none of this to May.

There is the joke about 'Marriage is a wonderful institution, but who likes institutions?' This is a very popular joke among crooks because institutions are an occupational hazard, so to speak, and everybody always jokes about what is most dear to the heart. Only when you are really married, I was finding out, it ain't such a joke. I no sooner got out of the jail on Riker's than May began to give me the business.

I hope you learned a lesson, she would say, and when are you going to quit, she would say, and didn't you see enough bums on Riker's, she would say, and finally we had a really big argument which was saved from becoming a beating by the telephone call from Mr Carfon. I swear to God, I was ready to knock her head against the wall if it hadn't been for that telephone call.

It started when I came around that night. It was about eight o'clock. She had found an apartment in the Bronx while I was away, and it was a nice little dump and she furnished it pretty good with the money Mr Carfon had gave me together with what we had managed to save. I got to say for Mr Carfon that the hundred and a quarter went to May every week like clockwork all the time I was away. I got to say for myself, too, that I'm a valuable man and he was probably figuring all that. Nobody gives nothing for nothing.

May was in the living room watching television when I came around. I sat down next to her and put my arm around her, and she just sat there and kept watching the program.

'What you doing?' I said.

'Watching television. What does it look like?'

She was wearing a sweater and slacks, and I have to admit she looked pretty good. I went to touch her, and she moved away from me.

'Don't, she said.

'What's the matter?'

'Nothing.'

'May,' I said, 'why don't we turn off the television and go in the other room?'

'I don't want to,' she said.

'Why not?'

'I don't.'

'Yeah. I heard you. Why not?'

'Because I don't like the work you're doing, and I've asked you a hundred times to quit, and you won't. And if you won't do anything for me, I sure as hell won't do anything for you.'

'Now don't be silly, baby,' I said. 'A husband – '

'I don't care what a husband – '

'A husband has rights!' I said.

'And so has a wife!' she said.

'A wife's rights don't include telling her husband how he should make a living.'

'All right, they don't,' May said. 'If that's the way you want it, fine. But don't expect anything from me because you're not going to get it.'

'Baby,' I said, 'I don't like the way you're talking. Any time I want anything, and I mean *any time*, and I mean *anything*, I'll get it. Now don't forget that.'

'Big man,' May said, and that was all she said.

I went to reach for her again, and she stood up and walked away. I caught her hand and pulled her back to the couch, and I grabbed for her sweater and started unbuttoning it, and she

117

twisted away and yelled, 'Leave me alone, goddamn you! Don't you understand? I don't want to have anything to do with you!'

I pinned her down to the couch holding one arm across her body. I grinned at her and said, 'Now that's too bad, May, because I want to have something to do with you,' and with my free hand I began unbuttoning her sweater all the way down while she wiggled and tried to get free. I got the sweater open, and then I grabbed her rough, just to let her know I wasn't taking any crap from her, and the minute my hand touched her breast she shoved me off, twisting her body and getting free and getting up off the couch. She turned to me with her eyes really flashing. She looked sexy as hell with the sweater open down the front, and the bra all twisted, and she yelled, 'You rotten son of a bitch! Leave me alone! Get an honest job, or leave me alone!'

That was when I got up off the couch ready to cave in her head.

That was when the phone rang.

I answered it, and Mr Carfon said, 'Frankie? Get over here right away.'

'Okay,' I said, and I hung up. I turned to May. 'This ain't finished, you know,' I said.

'Frankie, please,' she said, 'please don't let me hate you.'

Mr Carfon was pretty sore. I never seen him sore like that before. He was wearing a smoking jacket, and he kept walking up and down the room in front of the couch, mad as hell. There was a blonde on the couch. She had on a tight silk dress, and no shoes. Her legs were tucked up under her on the couch. She was a very expensive doll, you could see that just by looking at her. She was dressed the way I wanted to dress May, now what the hell kind of a way was that to behave? Didn't the stupid idiot know I loved her? Didn't she know I was doing what I knew how to do so that she could dress the way Mr Carfon's blonde on the couch was dressed? Dames, Jesus, I can't understand them.

This dame kept sipping at her drink all the while Mr Carfon paced in front of the couch. See no evil, hear no evil, speak no evil, that was this dame. All she knew from was sipping at her drink.

'I just received a telephone call,' Mr Carfon said, and the blonde didn't listen. She looked a little bored, as if this business had interrupted what was a pretty good party.

'Who from?' I asked.

'Andy Orelli,' Mr Carfon said.

'What's on his mind?'

'He wants to leave the organization,' Mr Carfon said. 'In fact, he *has* left the organization. He and Celia have rented a house in the Bronx. Apparently Celia's going to have a goddamned baby and Andy – '

'A baby!' I said, and I remembered the talk I had with her that day long ago.

'Yes,' Mr Carfon said. 'A baby.' He turned to the blonde. 'Louise, get out of here,' he said.

'Where do you want me to go?' the blonde asked.

'The bedroom, the office, the bathroom, I don't give a damn. Just go.'

The blonde swung her long legs over the edge of the couch. She didn't bother putting on her shoes. 'Nice meeting you,' she said to me, and I nodded. We both watched her as she trotted out of the room barefoot. Mr Carfon waited until the bedroom door closed behind her. I knew better than to make any comment about the blonde.

'A baby!' Mr Carfon exploded. 'Celia! Of all people!'

'Yeah,' I said.

'It upsets me because I didn't imagine Celia wielded such power, and it upsets me because I misjudged Andy. Also, there are further complications.'

'Like what?'

'Andy knows the workings of this organization quite well. He has seen our books, he is familiar with almost every phase of the operation, he is able to name dates and places and amounts, and he can identify almost every man in the outfit, including many out-of-town people. At the risk of sounding stereotyped I think it would be completely accurate to say "Andy knows too much." Do you understand me, Frankie?'

'Yes, Mr Carfon.' I didn't know what that sterophonic or whatever was, but the rest was pretty clear. Andy knew too much. Period. 'You want me to visit him and convince him he ought to stick around?'

'It's a little late for that. Celia seems to have convinced him that the righteous path is the true path, that being a father entails quitting a life of evil gain. I wouldn't have thought it possible, but . . . ' He shrugged.

'Well, what did you have in mind?' I said.

'You understand that he is a dangerous man to have roaming around as a free agent?'

'I understand.'

'You understand, too, that I have tried wherever possible in the past to avoid unnecessary violence?'

'That's right, Mr Carfon.'

'You'll remember what I said to you once, Frankie. I said I'd let you know when we could use your gun. We can use it now.'

I didn't say anything.

'I want Andy killed,' Mr Carfon said flatly. 'As soon as possible.'

I looked at him for a few seconds, and then I said, 'Okay.'

I walked around the streets a while before I went home. There's something about New York late at night that gets me. It's a real sad city late at night. There ain't many cabs in the streets, and the buses run only once in a while, and there are people coming home from places, and you don't see any lights on in the apartment buildings, except the lights in the small windows which are the bathrooms, and they only pop on every now and then and add to the sadness. You see a lot of drunks late at night, and they're sad as hell, especially the old women. I kept expecting to find my own mother in an alley some night, her stockings all rolled down and her dress all cockeyed. Jesus, that's depressing as hell. It's sad, too, to look in the all-night restaurants and see guys sitting all alone drinking coffee. That's very sad, I think, guys who have to drink coffee all alone at two o'clock in the morning.

I guess I was feeling pretty miserable that night. I couldn't understand what had happened between me and May, Jesus, I couldn't for the life of me understand it. We'd started out so fine, you know, until she began nagging at me about quitting a job which was bringing in real loot. I guess the Riker's Island bit had really snapped the cord. That had done it, all right. Before her husband was only a thief, sort of, but now he was also a jailbird. How could I explain to her that I was never going to jail again as long as I lived? How could I explain to her that all I was trying to do was get somewhere in the damn outfit? How could I even *talk* to her again after what she'd pulled tonight? What was I, a monster of some kind, she couldn't even stand to have me making love to her? What kind of an attitude was that, anyway? Man, I felt miserable.

I also felt miserable about another thing that was bothering me, and I guess it tied in with May harping on me all the time. She wanted me to quit, quit, quit. Okay, Andy Orelli had quit, quit, quit. And now Andy Orelli was slated for a coffin. So it wasn't as easy as that to just walk out. If Andy knew more than me about the operation, I still knew quite a bit about it. So what was I supposed to do? Even if I wanted to walk out – which I didn't – but which I maybe would have done to keep May happy, how could I? I not only was in up to my nostrils, but I was about to kill Andy, and then all I could do was hope that nobody made waves.

I guess it also bothered me that Mr Carfon had tapped me for the Andy kill. I mean, what the hell, I had nothing against the guy. But at the same time, I knew what it would mean with Andy out of the way. Somebody would have to move up. Either Weasel or me. And whereas it ain't a good thing to rat on another guy, I didn't see nothing wrong with going to Mr Carfon and telling him that Weasel had slugged me that night in the jewelry store. Mr Carfon would believe me. I knew he would. And he wouldn't take too kindly to Weasel – who cost him a lot of money when you figure lawyers and all – who'd conked me for his own personal gain. So I thought about May, and about leaving the outfit, and about having to kill Andy, and about what it would mean with him out of the way, but I felt pretty miserable. So I decided to go home.

May was waiting up for me.

She was wearing a nightgown and a bathrobe, and she was sitting in the kitchen with a cup of tea and she was crying. I went to the bathroom first, and then into the kitchen. I stood near the stove and I looked at her and said, 'What's the matter?'

She just shook her head and kept on crying.

'What are you drinking there?' I asked her.

'Tea,' she said.

'Is there any more?'

'There's hot water on the stove,' she said. 'And tea bags in the cabinet.'

I fixed myself a cup of tea and then sat down opposite her at the table. 'I hate to see guys sitting and drinking alone,' I told her. 'It makes me sad.'

'Yes.'

'I guess it's pretty good being married, huh? A guy comes home, he's always got somebody to sit down and have a cup of tea with, huh? Rawther, old bean, wot?' I said, trying to kid her out of it. 'Eh wot, old chap? Cup of tea, wot?'

'Yes,' she said.

'Come on. Dry up the tears. It ain't the end of the world.'

'I did a terrible thing tonight, Frankie,' she said.

'It was all right.'

'No. It wasn't.'

'We both got a little excited, so what?' I said.

'I feel like a . . . like a prostitute.'

'Hey, hey, come on. Now come on, cut it out. Don't talk like that about the girl I love. Drink your tea. Eh wot, old chap? Good tea, wot?'

'Frankie, Frankie,' she said, and she threw herself into my arms and almost knocked over the hot cup of tea. 'Forgive me, please. Please.'

'You're forgiven, okay?'

'But, Frankie, I'm so worried. I'm terrified. I thought I'd die when they put you away. Frankie, please, will you think about leaving Mr Carfon? Will you seriously think about it?'

'Sure, I will,' I said. 'But not right now. Okay?'

'Because I can't see it getting anything but worse, Frankie. The things you have to do, and the people you have to associate with. Don't you see? There's good in you, Frankie, and decency, and they're robbing it from you. And from me. I hated you tonight, Frankie. I hated you with every bone in my body.'

'So what? You *should* have hated me. I was a slob. What the hell kind of a way was that to behave, huh? What am I, a rape artist or something?'

'That's just it, Frankie. It wasn't you tonight, it was somebody else, the other person you . . . you can become. And I hated him. If you'd have touched me again, I'd have killed you, Frankie.'

'Ho, listen to the big murderer.'

'I'm serious.'

'Okay. I'm sorry, honey. It won't happen again, believe me. If you don't feel like it, I'll leave you al – '

'No, I don't want to be left alone. I want to love you. I want to give you all the love I have, Frankie.'

'Then we got no problem, right?'

'If you'll promise to think about it seriously. About leaving Mr Carfon. About getting a . . . a good job someplace. Where . . . where we can act normal and . . . and be normal.'

'Sure,' I said. 'I'll give it serious thought. I really will, May. Listen, are you finished with your tea?'

'Yes,' she said.

'Then why don't we hop off and get some crumpets, wot?'

'I really love you, you goof,' she said, and she kissed me, and so we made up that night, and I guess I really loved her, too. I guess I did.

10

It's hard to explain New York to somebody doesn't live there. It's so different from a small town, it's amazing. There are lots of people who say it's really only a big small town, but that ain't so. In a small town, the way it's laid out, there's usually just one big lighted section where there's the business district, and the movies, and the restaurants and like that. Once you leave the lighted section, you have your houses and that's the whole town. But in New York, it's different. New York is like a string of small towns, but none of the small towns is a town in itself. You put them all together, and you got New York. I'm not talking about the boroughs, of which there are five, and of which Brooklyn is the most famous, God knows why. But I'm talking about the various sections of the city. Like, for example, if you start all the way downtown, you got the Wall Street section which is a little town all by itself. Then the city quiets down, and there ain't much jumping until you hit the Fourteenth Street section further uptown, and then more quiet until you hit Thirty-fourth, and then Grand Central, and then Columbus Circle and then Seventy-second and then Eighty-sixth and like that all the way uptown.

The Bronx has its own spots of light, too, if you're familiar with that particular borough. In grammar school, the teachers in New York make sure you say *The* Bronx, and not just Bronx. If you're writing a letter, it's a big sin you should say *Bronx* and leave out the *The*. But in the Bronx you've got 149th and then Tremont Avenue and then Fordham Road and places like that where suddenly there's neons and a lot of people and movie houses and restaurants and ice-cream joints. That's the way New York is.

I'm explaining all this because I want you to understand

where Andy and Celia were living. They didn't live on Tremont or Fordham Road or the Grand Concourse or Mosholu or any of the pretty busy bustling areas. They lived up in the tail end of the East Bronx past Gun Hill Road. Gun Hill is a wide street, but it don't really class with Tremont or Fordham. It's got a new housing project now, and the church built a school, and there's Evander Childs High School a little further up the block, but Gun Hill Road is still a pretty quiet street, and they lived even past Gun Hill, up on 217th Street between Barnes Avenue and Bronxwood Avenue. They lived in a two-story frame house right opposite the junior high school. It was a very dark street at night, and a very quiet one.

There were front steps to the house, of course, and a wide driveway on the left of the house which led to the back steps. Andy and Celia lived on the second floor, and you had to climb a long flight of wooden steps to get up to the kitchen door. The people downstairs had a fig tree in the back yard. Nine out of ten times, if the owners of a house are Italian, you'll find they got a fig tree in the back yard. They cover it up with tarpaper in the wintertime. It looks ugly as hell. In the summer, it brings them a little piece of Italy, they should go back there they love it so much instead of planting trees which they cover with tarpaper and make look ugly in the winter.

There was a pretty strong wind the night I went to see Andy. I didn't get up to that part of the Bronx until about ten thirty. I was driving the car Mr Carfon had given me and I was driving carefully. I found the house without any trouble. I always had a good sense of direction, especially in New York where I know every street like I know the back of my hand. I parked the car right in front of the house, and then I got out and took my gloves from where they were on the seat and put them on. I had already checked the .45, so I knew there was a full magazine in it. I closed the car door and walked up the driveway to the back of the house and then up the rickety wooden steps. I had to hang on to the banister because the wind was very strong at the back of the house and it almost knocked me off the steps. That would have been too bad, getting knocked down that long flight of steps. There was a little landing at the top of the steps, a sort

125

of an open porch, maybe six feet by six feet with a little bench against the railing and a milk box near the steps. There was a storm door which I opened, and then there was the regular kitchen door with four panes of glass, and a shade pulled down inside. There was no light in the kitchen but there was a light coming from someplace in the house. I rapped on the glass.

There wasn't an answer right away, so I rapped again.

'Who is it?' Andy yelled, and then I could hear him coming into the kitchen.

'It's me, Andy,' I said. 'Frankie Taglio.'

'Who?'

'Frankie.'

'Oh,' he said, surprised. 'Oh, just a second, Frankie.' I could hear him walking through the apartment. I couldn't figure why until he opened the door. He was wearing a bathrobe, so I figured I surprised him in his underwear, and he went back to put something on. Nothing's as ridiculous as a guy in his underwear. Sometimes when I see the underwear ads, I almost bust out laughing even though they try to make the guy look glamorous in his shorts. It's impossible to make any guy look glamorous in his shorts, and that includes Rock Hudson and Elvis Presley and anybody. Put a guy in shorts, and he becomes ridiculous. So it was understandable why Andy went back to put on a bathrobe.

He seemed very happy to see me. He took my hand and said, 'Come in, Frankie. Boy, you're a sight for sore eyes.'

I went into the kitchen with him, and he locked the door behind me, and then we walked through to the living room. The apartment was a railroad flat, first the kitchen, then the living room, and then a closed door which I supposed went into the bedroom. The television set was going, but it was turned on very soft.

'I was watching the TV,' Andy said. 'What brings you around, Frankie?'

'Oh, I had an errand up around 238th,' I told him. 'I got done early and figured I'd take a chance maybe you was still up.'

'Gee, I'm glad you came,' Andy said. 'It's been very quiet.'

'Where's Celia?'

'She's in bed already.' He shrugged. 'You know. She's got a condition. Listen, you want something to drink? Glass of beer? Some wine?'

'What kind of wine you got?' I said.

'Dago red.'

'Good.'

He went back in the kitchen and took a bottle of wine from the refrigerator. He brought back two glasses also, and he poured for both of us. Before he sat down, he turned off the television.

'You like it chilled?' he said.

'Yeah, fine.'

He raised his glass. 'Well, here's luck.'

'Drink hearty,' I said, and we drank. It was good wine. I told him so.

'My father makes it,' Andy said. 'Every year, he makes it by hand. Hardly nobody bothers to do that any more, you know. But every year, those crates of grapes arrive, and the old man crushes them himself and puts the wine up in barrels in the basement of his house on a Hun' Twentieth. You got to give him credit. One year, he had the whole batch spoil, turn to vinegar, but that don't stop him. It's good wine, ain't it?'

'Yeah, it's very good.'

I don't know why I was sitting there throwing the bull with Andy, but I'll tell you the truth I didn't have much heart for the job. He wasn't looking good, Andy. He needed a shave, and he'd lost some weight and I, I don't know, he had the look of a guy who just hangs around the house all day doing nothing. I felt kind of sorry for him.

'What you been doing?' I asked him.

'Oh, you know.'

'You working?'

He shook his head. 'Not yet.'

'Why not?'

'Well, it ain't easy. I got a record, you know. I don't know if you knew that or not.'

'No, I didn't know.'

'Yeah, I done two years. This was right after Celia and me

127

was first married. I was just a kid at the time. I done it at Sing Sing, you ever see that joint?'

'No.'

'It's up the Hudson. It's quite a joint. Anyway, a guy finds out you're an ex-con, it ain't so easy to get a job. I almost got a job running an elevator downtown yesterday. It was a building on Eighteenth Street. But it didn't work out because the owner found out I got a record. It's rough, Frankie, believe me.'

'So why'd you leave the outfit?' I said.

'Well, what was I gonna do? You want more wine?'

'No. Thanks.'

'Have another glass.'

'All right. Just a little.' He poured, and I said, 'That's enough.'

'Celia's gonna have a baby, you know, and . . . well . . . you know you begin thinking a little about the future, I guess.' He shrugged.

'You can still come back,' I said.

He shook his head. 'No, I don't want to. No. I think I'm doing the right thing.'

'I think you're being foolish, Andy.'

'Ain't you never felt like starting a family, settling down?'

'Maybe,' I said.

'So how you gonna do it with the outfit? You got to raise kids decent, don't you?'

He looked sad as hell. I felt real sorry for him. I felt like going over and patting him on the shoulder or something. 'Listen,' I said. 'I wish you'd come back. I really wish you'd change your mind.'

'No . . . no, I couldn't.'

'Sure, you could. I could talk to Mr Carfon. I could tell him how you realized you made a mistake.'

'But I didn't,' Andy said. 'I didn't make no mistake. I done the right thing.'

'Oh, come on, Andy. You just now told me you can't even get a job.'

'I'll get one,' he said.

'Where? Doing what?'

128

'Someplace. I ain't proud. I'll do something. I'll clean out toilets if I got to.'

'That's a great job, all right. What the hell's the matter with you?'

'Nothing. I'm just looking forward to having the kid, that's all.'

How the hell can you kill a man when you're sitting with him drinking his wine and talking friendly? I began to realize I made a mistake. I should have let him have it when he opened the door. Now we'd been throwing the bull around and getting friendly and now it would be hard. How can you shoot a man when you ain't sore at him? Or when he ain't sore at you?

'I'm kind of hoping it'll be a boy,' Andy said.

'Yeah?'

'Yeah. I got all sisters in my family. Nobody to carry on the name. My father feels real bad about that. About my being the only son. If I don't produce some boys, bingo, there goes the line. So he's really banking on me. He's tickled Celia is pregnant.'

'Yeah? Maybe he shouldn't be so tickled.'

'What do you mean?' Andy said. 'You want some more wine?'

'No. Maybe when this baby is born, whether it's a boy or a girl or whatever, maybe you *still* don't carry on the family line.'

Andy looked at me puzzled. My face had changed, I guess. I guess he knew from my face that I wasn't being the buddy-buddy drinking wine with an old pal no more.

'What do you mean?' he said.

'Maybe the baby ain't yours,' I said.

He kept looking at me funny. Then he said, 'Then whose baby is it?'

'Mine,' I said, and the lie burned in my throat.

He was quiet for a long time, and then he just began chuckling softly. 'Come on,' he said. 'Cut it out.'

'That all you're gonna say?'

'Come on, I don't like this kind of kidding.'

'Goddamnit, I ain't kidding! Now how about it?' I got up. I was anxious to pull the gun. I was anxious for him to blow his stack and come at me. I was wasting too much time. This had to be done, and it had to be done now. 'I'm telling you it's my baby. Mine and *Celia's!*'

'Sit down,' Andy said. 'Cut it out.'

'You thick or something? Don't you understand? Your wife and me – '

'Sure, sure,' Andy said. 'Come on, have some more wine.'

'You goddamn jerk,' I yelled. 'Don't you know why I'm here?'

'No. Why are you here?'

'To kill you,' I said, and I pulled out the .45.

Andy looked at the gun and at the long silencer on the end of it. He looked up at my face then. His eyes were sad and sober and old.

'Put that away, Frankie,' he said, very softly.

'Give me a good reason,' I told him.

'A good reason is that you can't kill me. For Christ's sake, I'm your friend!'

'Are you?'

'Look, for God's sake – '

'Mr Carfon thinks you're dangerous. He thinks you got too much information in your head. He thinks you might drop something in the wrong place and down comes the house of cards. He thinks you'd be better off dead, Andy.'

'Come on,' he said, like an angry father with a kid. 'Put away that gun. Don't be stupid. Have another glass of wine. Come on, sit down.'

'No, Andy,' I said.

'Frankie, for – '

'No, Andy.'

'You ain't gonna kill me,' he said. 'If you don't know it, I do. You just ain't gonna kill me in cold – ' and I pulled the trigger.

There was a look of complete surprise on Andy's face. His mouth popped open, and his eyes went wide, and he said, 'Jesus, you – ' and I pulled the trigger again, and then again, the gun making small puffing sounds in the quiet living room, no explosions, only these funny little *poof* sounds. He grabbed at his chest, and the bathrobe came open when he fell, and he lay on the floor with blood all over the T-shirt, a ridiculous fat guy in his undershorts.

The door to the bedroom opened. Celia was standing in it. She was wearing a nightgown that swelled out over her belly. She really looked pregnant. She couldn't have been too far along yet, and still she looked more pregnant than almost any dame I ever seen. She looked at me, and at the gun in my hand, and she just gasped but she didn't say nothing. And then she walked to where Andy was laying dead on the floor, and she stooped down beside him, and she sort of touched his face gently, and then she stood up and looked at me. Her blonde hair was mussed from sleep. She didn't have no lipstick on.

'Get out, Frankie,' she said.

'Uh-uh,' I told her.

She looked at me. 'Get out.'

'You should have stood in bed,' I said.

'What do you –'

'You shouldn't have come out here and seen me, Celia. It would have been better the other way.'

Her eyes opened a little bit. She kept looking at me as if she couldn't believe what I was saying. And then I saw it come into her eyes. Fear. Stripped of everything human. Just fear. Just animal fear.

'I'm . . . I'm carrying a baby,' she said.

'I know.'

'You wouldn't –'

'Celia, you should have stayed in the other room.'

'I'm carrying a *baby!*' she pleaded.

'That's too bad, Celia.'

'Don't take away the one chance I ever –'

I fired twice. I fired for her head. The gun made two small sounds, and then she fell awkwardly to the floor and she was dead.

11

It wasn't so bad.

I slept all right that night. I sure as hell wasn't going to lose no sleep over anything that had to be done. And it had to be done, you better understand that or you'll have me all wrong. I'm no killer or nothing like that. What had to be done was done. I happened to be the guy picked for it. I didn't get no particular joy out of it, I'm not one of these crazy bastards who go around shooting people for kicks. It wasn't nothing like that, it was just something had to be done.

I didn't get up until about twelve o'clock the next day. I went in the kitchen in my pajamas. May was cleaning around.

'Hi,' I said.

She didn't answer me. She took the morning newspaper that was near the sink and slammed it down on the kitchen table. I didn't even look at it.

'Can I get some breakfast?' I said.

'You know where the cereal is, and there's coffee on the stove.'

'No juice?'

'In the refrigerator.'

I looked at her and then got my own breakfast. I couldn't help seeing the headline on the paper. It said GANGLAND SLAYING! I started drinking my juice, reading the story at the same time. They didn't have even the tiniest clue. They knew Andy Orelli was a racketeer with a record, but they couldn't figure why he was rubbed or even who would want him rubbed. In one of the columns, it said maybe it wasn't a gang killing at all. Maybe a burglar had come in or something. I closed the paper and finished my juice.

'Where were you last night, Frankie?' May asked.

'With the boys.'

'Is that your alibi?'

'Alibi? What the hell do I need an alibi for? I was playing cards with the boys. Check with any one of them. There were five guys in the game, and they'll all swear I was with them.'

'I'm not the police, Frankie. Save it for them.'

'What do I need to save anything for them?' I said. 'What are you talking about?'

She pointed to the newspaper. 'Did you do it?'

'Do *what*, for Christ's sake?'

'That . . . that killing!'

'Don't be ridiculous. I was playing cards last night.'

'Look at me, Frankie.'

I looked at her.

'Did you kill Andy and Celia?'

'No. Of course not.'

'I don't believe you.'

'So don't,' I said. 'Believe whatever the hell you want to. Only don't let me hear you ever thinking I'm involved with this, you hear? Not even thinking! I was playing cards with the boys last night. You just remember that.'

'I remember that you left the house at ten and you got back at twelve. The newspaper says Andy and Celia were killed a little after eleven.'

'You better remember that I left the house at nine and didn't get back until three. That's what you better get straight in your head.'

'Then you did kill them!' May said.

'I never killed nobody,' I told her, 'and I ain't starting now. Just remember what I said.'

'Frankie, Frankie . . . '

'I'm getting dressed. I got to go see Mr Carfon. Maybe I'll have good news when I get back.'

'What kind of news? A promotion? Into Andy's place? Into the place of the man you killed?'

'Cut that out, May. I'm not kidding you. You can get me in a lot of trouble by saying that. Cut it out.'

'You're just a no-good –'

'Shut up!' I said. She closed her mouth and stood staring at me as if she hated the sight of me. 'I'm getting dressed,' I said.

The news at Mr Carfon's place wasn't so hot. Not for me, anyway.

Jobbo was there when I arrived, and this new kid Georgie was there, too. Jobbo was busy on the phone, I don't know doing what. Georgie walked over to me as soon as I came in. He was a handsome kid, this Georgie, maybe nineteen years old, with brown eyes and a black pompadour. He was learning how to dress, too. I guess Mr Carfon laid a little cash on him for clothes. He came over and gave me the glad hand. He had a smile that looked as if he wasn't smiling. I don't know if you ever met anybody like that. He had very bright big teeth, and when he smiled it was as if he was purposely turning on a sign. What I mean is, it looked like he was smiling because he once read someplace that a guy can say whatever he wants to so long as he smiles when he says it. That way, he won't get rapped in the mouth as often. I don't know where he read it, but I hit plenty of guys who was smiling. They stopped smiling the minute I hit them.

'I read about your exploits,' he said.

'Yeah?'

'Nice work, Frankie.'

'Thanks.'

He was looking at my shirt. He kept looking at it, and then he said, 'I never before seen a button-down shirt with French cuffs.'

'I have them made,' I said.

'Is that expensive?'

'Pretty expensive.'

He nodded, and then looked as if he wanted to reach out and touch the shirt, if you know what I mean. I got a feeling he had itchy hands. I turned him off right away before he decided to get buddy-buddy. Jobbo was just getting off the phone, so I went over to talk to him. We didn't have much to say to each other. It's always been my opinion that there's nothing deader than a dead friendship – and Jobbo and me wasn't even very good friends to begin with. So we just talked about nothing, but it was better than talking with Georgie over there.

After a while, Mr Carfon came out of the office with Milt. They both came over to me and shook my hand.

'Good job, Frankie,' Mr Carfon told me.

'Thanks.'

'I think a little bonus might be in order, don't you, Milt?'

'I sure do,' Milt said. 'What happened with Celia?'

'She seen me.'

'Too bad,' Milt said.

'Yes,' Mr Carfon said. 'No police have been to your home?'

'No.'

'I doubt if they will. A bonus for Frankie, Milt. He's earned it.'

'Is that all I earned?' I said.

'What do you mean, Frankie?'

'There's a hole, ain't there?'

Mr Carfon smiled. 'Still the ambitious one,' he said. 'Ah, Frankie, Frankie, will you never learn patience? There is such a thing as precedence, you know that, don't you?'

'I don't know what "precedence" means.'

'It means first come, first serve,' Milt said.

'Yeah? And what does that mean?'

'It means that certain people have been in this organization longer than you have, Frankie,' Mr Carfon said. 'You are, after all, a comparative newcomer.'

'Who are you talking about?' I said.

'Weasel,' Mr Carfon said.

'He gets Andy's spot, huh?'

'Yes.'

'That's great. A punk like Weasel –'

'Now, Frankie . . .'

'Who slugged me from behind on that jewelry store caper?'

'Frankie, Frankie . . .'

'Don't you believe me? I'm telling you what happened. Weasel slugged me and left me for the cops. That's a guy to trust, huh?'

'I think he can be trusted, Frankie.'

'So why didn't you send *him* to take care of Andy?'

'Because I sent *you*, Frankie. Do you have any objections?'

'Yes, Mr Carfon, I do. I'm sorry, but I do. I think you're making a mistake with Weasel. I don't think he can be trusted, and I also think I'm a better man than he is, and to tell you the truth, I'm sore.'

'Try Vaseline,' Milt said, and he laughed.

'Don't get wise, Milt,' I said.

'What?'

'You heard me.'

'None of that,' Mr Carfon said. 'Frankie thinks he has a legitimate beef, and he voiced it. I see no reason for ridicule.'

'Thanks, Mr Carfon,' I said, 'but that don't change the situation none. Weasel is *still* over me.'

'Yes.'

'Well, I don't like it.'

'Well, that's unfortunate. But I couldn't very well ignore a man who has worked hard and long and well. Whatever happened in the jewelry store is a matter of conflicting opinions. I trust you both, but obviously I must believe either one or the other of you.'

'And you believe him, huh? You think I'm a big clumsy jerk who goes tripping into display cases, huh?'

'I think nothing of the sort, Frankie. I prefer to forget the entire incident rather than being forced into the position where I must disbelieve one of you. The jewelry store incident played no part whatever in my choice of Weasel as the logical successor to Andy.'

'Logical, huh?' I said. 'I don't see much logic in that.'

'You'll have to, for the present,' Mr Carfon said. 'Have I ever made any false promises to you, Frankie?'

'No, but – '

'All right. I said you would one day be a big man, and you will. There's plenty of room at the top, Frankie. Plenty. Just learn to be a little more patient.'

'Yeah,' I said.

'Would you like a drink?'

'No.'

'Very well. But do believe me when I say there'll be a lot more coming your way.'

'Sure.'

'Just learn to wait for it.'

'Sure.'

'I have a job for you this week end. I thought perhaps I'd send you and this new boy, Georgie. He's going to go places, that boy. Do you feel up to it?'

'Whatever you say. What kind of a job is it?'

'Nothing very important.'

'Then why don't you send the hot-shot Weasel?'

'Would you prefer that, Frankie?'

'I'll do whatever you say. That's what I'm supposed to do, ain't it?'

'Ah, Frankie, Frankie, you're still angry. All right, I'll send Weasel. But only because you did such a splendid job last night, and because I think you've earned a rest. All right?'

'Fine.'

'I wasn't kidding about that bonus. Milt?'

Milt fished into his wallet and handed me a bill. It was a C-note. Some bonus. Mr Carfon put his arm around my shoulder and said, 'Frankie, learn to be patient. Learn to wait.'

As it turned out, I didn't have to wait very long.

On Saturday night, I had another fight with May, this time on the way home from the movies. We were living in one of those quiet sections of the Bronx, near Fordham Road but in one of the side streets off Poe Park. We had gone to Loew's Paradise, which is right on the Grand Concourse, and then I took her for ice cream, and we were walking through the park, which is a short cut we took any time we weren't using the car, when she started in on me again. I really didn't feel like an argument. We were passing the thing where the bands used to play when I was a kid. We used to come up from Harlem to hear the bands. This was when I was around sixteen or so. They used to have dancing. You could always pick up a girl there. It was kind of fun. Anyway, it was a good memory to have, and I didn't feel like getting into no damn argument with May. But she started in about the Andy thing again, and before you knew it we were right in the middle of a major battle. So I left her right there in the park to walk home by herself, and I caught a cab and went downtown, figured I'd see what the boys were doing. I didn't mind not having the car with me because I always like to ride in cabs, anyway. When I was a kid, we used to play a game with cabs. We used to stand near the curb on First Avenue and wait for a cab to go by, and then we'd yell, 'Taxi! Hey, Taxi!' and those goddamn cabs would scream to a stop, and we'd go run in the hallway. One time, a cab driver chased us all the way up to the roof, he was so burned up. Those were the things we used to do.

Well, I got down to Harlem and it was pretty quiet for a Saturday night. I was tempted to ask the cabbie for change of the C-note, just to see his eyes bug. I mean, what the hell, have *you* ever seen a hundred-dollar bill? But I didn't. I just paid him and tipped him, and then walked around to see what was doing. I met Jobbo, and he was very excited. He was all bundled up in a heavy winter coat, I guess so he could sweat better. He was the kind of guy, his personality was ruined if he couldn't sweat. He came puffing down the street all excited, and he said, 'Did you hear, Frankie? Did you hear?'

'Did I hear what?'

'About the close shave with the cops?'

'What the hell are you talking about?'

'Weasel and Georgie. On this liquor-store holdup.'

'What happened?'

'The law showed while they were in the store. There was a big gun battle. It's on all the radios. Georgie got away fine.'

'And Weasel?' I said.

'I only got this from Georgie. But as they were running away, one of the cops clipped him.'

'Clipped Weasel?'

'Yeah. He's dead, Frankie.'

So there I was.

12

I talked to Georgie the next day, before I got the signal from Mr Carfon. He didn't seem to remember too much about how Weasel got it. Apparently they was in the liquor store and a uniformed cop showed up, and the owner yelled. Weasel opened fire. For a while there, Georgie thought they'd never get out of the store. But they finally managed it, with Weasel leading and Georgie running behind him. And then the cop's slug took Weasel, and Georgie just kept running. This is where the story was a little vague. The newspapers reported that the cop had been shot before the pair left the liquor store, so I couldn't understand how this cop, who'd been shot in the chest and who probably wasn't feeling much like fighting any more, had managed to pick himself up and take a good deadly aim on Weasel. But that's what Georgie said happened. I wasn't asking too many questions. If he was the one gave it to Weasel, I should have thanked him because that very afternoon I was Number Three in the outfit.

There was only Mr Carfon, Milt Hordzig, and me.

Number Three.

Me. Frankie Taglio.

I can't tell you how I felt that afternoon. First of all, I went to about four bills a week, which ain't potatoes, my friend. Second, I was a pretty big man now, though not so big as Milt, but pretty big. And I done it all in a very short time. I was somebody, do you follow me? At last I was somebody. And maybe you think it's funny that I wanted to tell my mother about it first, but that's who I wanted to tell.

So I went back to the old building in Harlem, and I climbed the steps like I must have done ten thousand times when I was a kid. I stopped outside the door, and I knocked, and my mother said, 'Come in.'

I went into the living room. She wasn't drunk. She was just sitting on the sofa and staring across at the small window where outside you could see the dirty brick wall of the next building.

'Hello, Ma,' I said.

'Frankie?'

She turned and looked at me. I hadn't seen her for a long time, not since May and me moved up to the Bronx. I'll tell you, like every time I seen her before, it was painful. This time, it was different. She was sober this time, and she looked a little bit – just a very little bit – like her old self.

I sat down alongside her on the sofa.

'How you been, Ma?' I said.

'Fine,' she answered. 'I get tired a lot, but I'm fine.'

My mother speaks fine English, even though she's Italian. In fact, she ain't really Italian. She was born right here in New York City. It was my father who was born in Naples, which makes him a real ginzo if he was still alive.

'How's May?' my mother asked.

'She's fine,' I said.

'She's a good girl.'

'Yes,' I hesitated. 'Ma, the reason I came around, I wanted to tell you I got a promotion today.'

My mother nodded.

'I'm getting four hundred dollars a week now, Ma,' I said.

'That's a lot of money.'

'It sure is,' I said.

'And all you have to do to earn it is kill people,' my mother said.

For a minute, I didn't answer her. Then I said, 'Aw, where'd you get that?'

'May was here.'

'When?'

'Yesterday, the day before. I don't remember.'

'What the hell did she want?'

'She asked me to talk to you. She asked me to tell you to quit.'

'She's crazy,' I said. 'Jesus, what the hell is wrong with her?' I hesitated again. 'What'd you say to her?'

'I told her I don't have a son,' my mother said. 'I told her you haven't listened to me since the time you were ten, and there was no reason to think you would now.'

'Aw, that ain't true,' I said.

'I never touched a drop since she came to see me,' my mother said. 'She told me you killed Andy Orelli and his wife . . . '

'For Christ's sake!'

'A man who grew up here in the neighborhood. Him and his pregnant wife. She said you killed them, Frankie.'

'She's nuts!'

'That's what she said you did. And when she left, I began to wonder. My Frankie a killer. A murderer. It made *me* feel like a murderer, Frankie. It made me feel as if *I* killed that poor man and his wife.'

'Don't believe what May tells you. For Christ's sake, do I look like a killer?'

My mother looked at me long and hard.

And then she said, 'Yes.'

'Me? Me, Ma? This is Frankie! Now come on, don't talk like that. I'm making a lot of money now. I'll be able to get you a nice place to stay, and nice clothes and – '

'I don't want anything from you,' my mother said.

'What kind of a way is that to talk to your own son, Ma? Just because – '

'I have no son,' she said.

'Ma, come on . . . '

'Do you know what I wish, Frankie?'

'What?'

'I wish you get hit by a car. I wish you get hit by a car and killed.'

'Ma, Mama,' I said. 'Mama, please don't talk like – '

'Go, Frankie,' she said. 'Go. I don't want to look at you. Not after what you done. I don't want to look at you.'

'Ma . . . '

'Go.'

I got up. 'Okay,' I said. I went to the door. At the door, I turned and very nasty I said, 'You want me to send up a bottle of cheap booze? Would that make you feel a little more cheerful, Mama dear?'

'A killer,' she said.

'Yeah, and a *drunk*,' I said, and I walked out.

I felt pretty miserable. I can never figure out dames, I swear to God. No matter what you try to do for them, they always turn out to be bitches. But I still felt pretty miserable. You'd think a guy's own mother would be a little happy when he started to get someplace. Instead, she came on with that killer crap. What the hell, I ain't a killer! Jesus, don't people know the difference?

I walked around the streets feeling rotten. I didn't want to go home to May because I knew she'd start the same crap my mother had given me. Where the hell was I supposed to go?

Around five o'clock, just when it began getting dark, I ran into Angelo. I hadn't seen him in a long time. He's a guy, Angelo, who had one eye shot out when he was a kid. Some bastard just jumped him and gave it to him with a zip gun, that was Angelo. He's been looking for that guy ever since, but he ain't found him yet. When he does, that guy is going to be sorry he was born. He's got a glass eye now, Angelo, and he walks with his head sort of cocked to one side. I guess because he can only see out of that one good eye. When I ran into him, he was very respectful. We used to kid around a lot, you know, but this time it was different. I swear, I expected him to start calling me Mr Taglio.

'Well, it certainly is a wonderful thing that happened to you,' he said. He has a very high whiney voice, Angelo. I notice that a lot of guys with physical defects, their voices get kind of whiney even though they never complain much.

'Yeah, it's a great thing,' I said.

'What are you doing down here in Harlem?'

'I came to see my mother.'

'She must be happy,' Angelo said.

'Yeah, she's tickled.'

'Are you going home now?'

'No. I don't feel like going home.'

Angelo was quiet for a long time as if, now that I was sort of a big shot in the organization, he was sort of ashamed to ask me. But then, he finally did.

'Is there . . . ah . . . anything I can do for you, Frankie?'

'What do you mean?'

'A girl.'

'Maybe,' I said.

We were both quiet for a couple of minutes.

'Nothing cheap,' I said.

'Nothing cheap,' he told me. 'Something special. Private stock. You're no punk, Frankie, I should give you something cheap.'

'I mean . . . I want a girl with class.'

He opened his wallet and took out a scrap of paper. He scribbled an address on it. 'Go down here,' he said. 'The – '

'I don't want no whorehouse.'

'No, no, this is where the girl lives. It's a very nice place, Frankie. On Sixty-eighth. Near Hunter College. Do you know where that is?'

'Yeah.'

'Go there. I'll call her. You'll like this girl. She has class.'

'Thanks,' I said.

'Anything for you,' Angelo said, 'let me know. Carte blanche for you, Mr Carfon said.'

I drove down to Sixty-eighth and couldn't find no parking spot. I finally parked on Third Avenue and Sixty-fifth and then I walked over to Sixty-eighth. The girl lived between Madison and Fifth. It was a nice brownstone, clean. I rang the bell and then walked up to the third floor. She answered the door. She was private stock, all right. She was the long-legged honey blonde who was in the apartment that night with Mr Carfon.

'Mr Taglio?' she said. 'Angelo called. I've been expecting you.'

We went into the apartment. Her name was Louise – what a crazy name for a girl who was built like her and who could do the things she did. I spent four days with her. I didn't want to leave that apartment, believe me. In that apartment, I was *Mister* Taglio. With my mother, I was a bum and a killer. With May, I'd have to listen to that whole routine again. But with this girl, for four days, I was somebody. I'd gone out and slain the dragons, and now I was the knight coming back to the castle,

143

that was it. There's only one trouble. You got to go home some-time. So at the end of the four days, I went home.

May said, 'Where've you been?'

'What difference does it make?'

'I want to know.'

'Go to hell,' I said. 'I been out of town.'

'Killing somebody else?'

'Here we go again, folks,' I said.

'Yes, here we go again. Listen to me, Frankie. I'm going to tell you something which I hope penetrates.'

'Save your breath.'

'I will. After this. But right now I want you to hear me. I'm asking you to quit Mr Carfon. I'm ask – '

'Do we have to go over all this again? I got a raise. Four hundred dollars a week. How does that sound to you?'

'Money doesn't matter, Frankie.'

'No, huh? You people who say money doesn't matter kill me. It matters, all right. It matters a whole hell of a lot.'

'Not to me it doesn't.'

'Well, to me it does.'

'I want you to quit Mr Carfon. I want you to get an honest job, and I want you to start working at our marriage. That's what I want, Frankie.'

'You finished?'

'Yes. Doesn't our marriage mean anything to you? Isn't there anything you think worth saving?'

'This is all in your head. There's nothing wrong with what I'm doing. You know it, and I know it.'

'Oh, Frankie. Please. For God's sake . . . '

'For God's sake, shut up,' I said. 'Would you rather be married to some bum who runs an elevator? Sixty bucks a week and a big fifty-dollar Christmas bonus? Is that what you want?'

'Yes. Better that. Better than to be married to a – '

'Don't say it, May. I'm warning you.'

'And I'm warning you, Frankie. I'm not asking you. I'm warning you. Either quit, or you'll be sorry.'

'Don't talk through your asshole,' I said.

'I'm warning you, Frankie.'

'Sure.'

'All right,' she said. 'You'll be sorry. Believe me. You'll be sorry.'

'I'm sorry I came home, that's for sure. If I hear another inch of this crap I'll go out of my mind. Dames never know when to shut up, do they?'

'No,' May said. 'Dames only know how to talk.'

'Well, you talk to the walls,' I said. 'I'm getting out of here.'

'Where are you going?' she said.

'Out.'

And I went.

I was thinking of buzzing Louise again, get lost with her for a month, a year, two years, just get lost with that honey blonde and her soft voice and that 'Mister' look in her eyes. I drove downtown thinking I might run into Angelo. I wanted to check with him first. I'd feel like a horse's ass just busting in on her in case there was some other guy there. I walked all around Harlem. There'd been a rumble. Some PR's from Spanish Harlem had come down and said something funny to one of the neighborhood girls. All the guys in the neighborhood had piled on the PR's and beat hell out of them. The place was swarming with cops. Everywhere you turned, there was another cop. I was carrying the .45, and I didn't want none of the cops to stop me and start frisking. So I steered a real wide path around them, and then finally I ran into Max. He was so high, he was doing Pepsi-Cola commercials up in the sky.

'Hello, Frankie,' he said. 'Ohhhhhh boy, you're a big man now, huh?'

'When you gonna knock off on that junk, Max?' I said.

'Shhh, shhh, man,' he said. 'There is all kinds of cops around here tonight. You see what the kids done to them PR's?'

'No. What?'

'They got them with ball bats. Oh, man, I never saw so many busted heads in my life. It was like a massacre. They came down on them PR's from all directions at once. Wham! Bam! Alacazam! Blood all over the sidewalk. You know something else?'

'What?'

'Them PR's couldn't even talk English. That dame who said they insulted her was full of crap. What happened was they got lost and was trying to find their way back to Spanish Harlem. They probably all three of them just come over here from Puerto Rico.'

'They should stay where they belong,' I said. 'I don't like people who can't speak English.'

'Could your father speak English when he came here?' Max said.

'Don't get wise, Max, or I'll use a ball bat on *you*.'

'I was only asking.'

'Never mind asking. I don't have to take crap from a junkie,' I said.

Every place I turned there was somebody with a lecture lately. It was getting to be something of a pain. How far up did you have to go before people got off your back? I decided right then and there that no matter how far it was, I was going the distance. Where I was was fine. But I wanted to be where punks like Max would take off their hats when I came down the street. I wanted to be where May would know she couldn't talk to me like that even if she *was* my wife.

I wanted to be on top.

And only Milt Hordzig stood in my way.

Or so I thought that night.

13

It was March already. That's my worst month. In March, I got no use for anything. Nobody in New York got any use for March. It's an in-between month. It ain't winter and it ain't spring. You don't know what to wear, and you don't know how to act. It's miserable. One thing I learned about New Yorkers is that they like things black or white. None of this gray jive. And, man, March is the grayest.

It was also very cold that March, and I never liked cold weather either. This comes from when I was a kid, I guess, and I never had clothes which were heavy enough to keep me warm. It made me laugh, this movie they showed about the GI's freezing in Korea. That's the way it was with me all the time I was a kid, and the movie guys tried to make it a hardship for the soldiers. Well, maybe it was a hardship for some big-mouth Texan who always had a sheep-lined jacket around him. But for me it would have been duck soup because, to put it plain, I was always freezing my ass off.

This March I had a camel-hair overcoat. It cost me two hundred dollars in Leighton's on Broadway which is where all the movie stars shop. I also had a blue cashmere sports jacket and three suits, and more ties than I could count, and two dozen tailor-made shirts, and socks made of 100 per cent wool. I had four pairs of shoes. A pair of black loafers, a pair of brown loafers, a dressy pair of black shoes, and a pair of high-top suède shoes which is like the British officers wear in India. I got a thing for cuff links and tie clasps, so I bought up thirty pairs of them. I spent a whole day doing it. I went from store to store picking out the sets. I didn't buy nothing for May because we weren't talking.

I went down to see Louise once. It was good.

The next day, I got a call from Mr Carfon. I thought maybe it was about Louise. I thought maybe he was going to tell me this was private stock, and I should lay off. But it wasn't.

There were three accountants with Mr Carfon and Milt when I got there. The way this worked, you see, Mr Carfon was no dope. He wasn't going to fool around with no possible income-tax-evasion rap for which they can lock you up and forget they ever had a key. In the United States of America, it is an accepted thing that you cheat on the income-tax allowances. Otherwise, man, you can't stay in business. What it is, if you spent forty dollars to entertain an out-of-town client, you mark it down as four hundred dollars. When they inspect the form, they will maybe disallow two hundred of that. You're still a hundred and sixty dollars ahead of the game. Nobody goes to jail for padding the allowances. The way you can go to jail is by not declaring income you received. Naturally, if you don't declare the income that means you ain't paying any tax whatsoever on it. This is how you can go to jail.

Mr Carfon didn't want to go to jail. Who does? But at the same time, he couldn't declare he made like a hundred thousand dollars importing heroin, and like fifty thousand dollars hustling dames, and twenty-five thousand from burglaries and holdups and such. So he had to have a front. And instead of one front, he had a lot of them, and everybody in the organization was a salaried man working for one of the fronts. For example, he had an import-export company, and he also had a couple of magazines, and an investment firm, and a trucking company. For the magazines, he hired a couple of legitimate jerks who just got out of Harvard or one of the other dumps, and they were the editors of the magazines and they didn't know there were about forty or fifty guys listed in the promotion department and the advertising department and the sales department, all drawing salaries from the handful of magazines the two jerks legitimately put out every month. The magazines maybe sold four copies each whenever they were put on the stands. The two Harvard jerks didn't realize this. They thought they were editing some of the fastest-selling, hottest little publications in America. Which is where the accountants came in, and which is

148

where my understanding of income tax gets fuzzy. But apparently it's all right to lose money on some enterprises, in fact sometimes it's wonderful for tax purposes to lose money. The whole thing in America, you see, is figuring out how you can get to keep twelve dollars out of the three-and-a-half million you earned last year. It is very unfair to the rich, but I say the hell with them.

Anyway, it took a lot of work to keep all those books for all those phony operations looking like the books for real operations. In other words, it was a complete fake. One dummy corporation did business with another dummy corporation. What it was, everybody was a crook, and the books made him honest. Mr Carfon paid the accountants a lot of money each year because it was them, so to speak, who kept him out of jail.

Well, they were there when I arrived. They looked like three monks making corrections on those big dusty manuscripts the monks work on. Mr Carfon gave me the big hello, so it wasn't about Louise after all. Milt came over and slapped me like I was his uncle from Jersey City he hadn't seen since the day he got *bar-mitzvahed*. Everything was palsy-walsy, jollsy-wollsy, and I began to wonder what was in the wind. We sat around and drank a little bit and yokked it up, but nobody was saying anything important. After a while, one of the accountants called Mr Carfon aside, and they had a private chat in the corner, both wagging their heads like doctors agreeing where to make the incision. Then Mr Carfon came over to me. Mr Carfon don't mince words, I like that about him. He's got something to say, he says it – with no bull.

'How would you like to move up, Frankie?' he said.

'You know I would,' I said.

'Up to now,' Mr Carfon said, 'I thought it advisable to limit the executive power of the organization to two men and only two men. I've just discussed the tax situation with our good Mr Knowles, and he tells me we have some money it would do well to disburse.'

'I'm not sure I understand,' I said.

'Then I'll explain it to you, Frankie. The money is in excess of forty thousand dollars a year. If I don't give it to someone

149

in the form of a salary, I'll have to give it to the government.'
Mr Carfon smiled. 'I hate giving anything to the government.'

'So?'

'So I'd rather give it to you.'

'Forty grand a . . . '

'Yes.'

I whistled. I was stunned, to tell the truth. I was lucky I could get the whistle out.

'Naturally, a salary of such magnitude would necessitate enlarging your status with the group. In short, were you to receive this salary, I would expect a sort of executive board. The members of the board would be Milt, me, and you.'

'I . . . I see,' I said. My palms were wet. I had a feeling my upper lip was wet, too, but I didn't make a move to wipe it.

'What do you think, Frankie?' Mr Carfon said.

'I . . . I think it's great. It sounds great.'

'And patience is its own reward, isn't it?' Mr Carfon said, laughing, and then all of a sudden he stopped laughing. 'There's just one problem,' he said. He had walked away from me, and now he turned to face me, and he looked very serious.

'What's that, Mr Carfon?' I asked. I was beginning to get a little nervous. That forty grand was almost in my mitt, and I didn't want nothing to come between us. 'What's that?' I said again.

'I had a visit yesterday,' Mr Carfon said. 'A little surprise visit.'

'From who?'

'From your wife.'

'May?' I said.

'Yes.'

'May came here? What did she – '

'She's a lovely girl, Frankie. Very pretty. She's also very tough. A lot of American pioneer spirit in that girl. It's a pity she was born a century too late.'

'Wh . . . what did she want?' I said.

'In effect, she wanted me to fire you.'

'Fire me? Oh, Jesus, why can't she – '

150

'I have no intention of firing you. I'm sure you know how much I think of you, Frankie. You're a valuable man. God knows, there are few enough around right now. With the exception of this new boy, Georgie, I don't see very much talent around. So I have no intention of firing you. Besides, as was the case with Andy, you know quite a bit about the organization's internal machine. I would like you to stay *inside* the organization.'

'I see,' I said. I didn't miss his point. He was saying: You better stay in the organization or you'll be shaking hands with Andy and Celia soon. 'Well, I got no intention of leaving,' I said, 'no matter what May thinks.'

'That's an admirable attitude, Frankie, admirable. Unfortunately, May is a tough girl with pioneer spirit. She has other ideas.'

'Ideas? What do you – ?'

'She has a rather outmoded sense of justice. She believes in crime and punishment. She thinks policemen are here to protect the citizenry.'

'Protect the – ?'

'Yes. To make this short, Frankie, she threatened to go to the police unless I release you.'

'The cops? May? Jesus, Mr Carfon, I can't believe – '

'Then ask her,' Mr Carfon said. 'You might be interested to know that she plans to tell them about the Andy Orelli incident. In short, Frankie, her threat is not an idle one. And whereas I've no doubt we can handle ourselves with the police department, I simply do not care to get involved. I've gone to great pains to establish a legitimate-seeming group of enterprises. A police investigation might possibly penetrate the front, and I wouldn't want that to happen. I might add that were you to be pulled in on the Orelli kill, I couldn't guarantee beating the rap for you and jeopardizing the organization. You'd be on your own. These are all things for you to consider.'

'But if she loves me so damn much, why would she want to send me to jail? Maybe the chair even?'

'To save you.' Mr Carfon smiled. 'To save you from yourself and – to use a favorite expression of the police – your "bad associates." Women sometimes act peculiarly, Frankie. None-theless, the facts remain.'

'What's her plan?'

'She wants you to quit by April first. That's only a week away, Frankie. If you have not left the organization by that time, she will go to the police. That's the long and the short of it.'

'I see.'

'Now, I don't know what emotional involvements you have with this woman. It's been my experience that women are like streetcars, but of course I'm older than you and, if you'll forgive me, somewhat wiser. Should you choose to leave the organiz-ation because of your attachment to this particular woman ...' Mr Carfon shrugged, and I thought of Andy again. 'On the other hand, should you remain with the organization, your wife presents a clear and recognizable danger. I'm presenting all the facts to you, Frankie, so that you can make your own decision. I don't want to force a choice upon you. And one of the facts is that if you remain with us, you will share the command with Milt and myself at a salary of ...' He turned to Knowles, the accountant. 'What was that, Richard?'

'Forty-two five,' the accountant said.

'Forty-two thousand five hundred dollars a year,' Mr Carfon said. 'If you stay. If you leave ...' Again he shrugged.

'Well ... well, what the hell am I supposed to do?' I said. 'If May's got this bug in her – '

'She does, believe me.'

'I'll beat the crap out of her,' I said.

'A temporary measure at best. And it might serve to strengthen her resolve.'

'Well, what – ?'

'Frankie, I don't have to tell you what an opportunity this represents. You'll be a big man, Frankie, a really big man. I'm not kidding you. And believe me, it isn't easy to come by this kind of a position or this kind of a salary these days. A big man, Frankie.'

'Yeah ...'

'The decision is yours,' he said. 'Think it over.'

'Yeah.'

'But not too long. She's going to the police on April first.'

I beat her up that night.

I swear to God, I beat her until she was limp. It didn't do no good. I couldn't understand her. She kept telling me she loved me and all that, but she wouldn't change her mind. Either I quit the goddamn outfit, or she'd go to the police. I tried to explain to her that you just don't walk out on something this big, did she think I was playing marbles on the street corner? She told me I only had myself to blame for the situation I was in, and either I quit or she'd go to the police. That was her song. Over and over again she sang it, and I beat the crap out of her.

The weather turned mild that week. Spring was in the air. New York was coming alive again. You could feel it. I swear to God you could just feel people beginning to take deep breaths in their lungs. I wish I could have enjoyed it. But all the time I walked in the streets, I kept thinking of May and me and the outfit. Forty grand a year. More than that. Forty-two five. That was a lot of money. I could do a lot with that money. If only May would be reasonable, we could live like a royal couple, that was the truth. Only May wouldn't be reasonable. May was a dame, and who can ever figure dames? Like streetcars, Mr Carfon had said. You miss one, and there was always another one right after that.

And yet, May wasn't like that. May wasn't no damn streetcar. May was my wife, don't a guy owe something to his wife? But don't he owe something to himself, too? For all the winters he froze his ass off? For being hungry? For being dead the first twenty years of his life? Don't he owe that much to himself? Don't he owe it to himself to grab what he can get, all he can get? Jesus, what the hell was a guy supposed to do?

And what would happen if I quit?

I knew what would happen. Mr Carfon played it safe and played it cool. If I quit, May would still be a danger to the outfit. And so would I. No, no there was no sense to that.

So what was I supposed to do?

April first was a Monday.

On Sunday night, May went to the movies alone. She wore dark glasses because to tell you the truth I'd hurt her real bad that night I beat her up, and her eyes didn't look good. I clocked her when she left the house, and then I called the Paradise to find out what time the show broke. They told me. I sat down to wait.

About a half-hour before she was supposed to leave the movie house, I went out. I went to Poe Park because I knew she'd take the short cut on the way home. I stood behind the thing where the bands used to play when I was a kid. It was a nice night, but there weren't many people in the park. It didn't matter anyway.

She came into the park around midnight. The park was almost empty by then. There was just an old guy sitting on a bench near the street lamp on the other end, reading a Yiddish newspaper. I guess I knew it the minute she entered the park, even though I couldn't see her face. She was wearing high heels, and I heard them on the concrete walk, and I watched her and the sway of her hips, and I pulled the .45 out of my waist band, and I put the silencer on the end of it, and my hand was sweating. I flipped off the safety.

I saw May when she passed the band stand. She walked with her head up, still wearing the dark glasses. I waited until she passed me.

And then I whispered, 'May.'

She turned. For a second, I thought she was going to smile, as if I'd surprised her by waiting to walk home with her.

I shot her four times, and then I ran away without looking back at her, and I threw the .45 down a sewer on the Concourse.

14

We didn't have the party until a month later.

The cops were finished with me by that time. They knew I had a record, you see, on a gun offense at that, and so they were pretty rough with me. But Mr Carfon set up an airtight alibi with the boys in Utica. There were a dozen guys upstate who swore that I was nowhere near New York City that night. Still, they kept at me until they realized they weren't going to get a thing out of it, and then they dropped it. They figured, I guess, that she was a punk's wife after all – so why waste too much time over her? Good riddance to bad rubbish is what they figured.

The party was a very big one. There were guys from out-of-town and everything. Mr Carfon introduced me all around. I was like the guest of honor. The whole party was to explain to everybody that I was a big man in the outfit now. There was liquor and food and girls. It was a crazy party.

I spotted Georgie there. He was wearing a tailor-made suit. Along around midnight, Mr Carfon brought him over to me and said, 'Frankie, I want you to keep your eye on this boy. He's going to be all right. He's going to be a big man.'

Our eyes locked, mine and Georgie's. He smiled at me. 'I want to congratulate you,' he said. 'It's a great thing.' He kept smiling.

'Thanks,' I said, but I didn't smile back.

It was a crazy party. I went home around two o'clock. Most of the guys stayed, but I went home. I was still living in the Bronx, even though I could afford a better place now. I thought I'd wait until the cops really buried whatever they had on me.

The apartment was very quiet. I went in, and then locked the door behind me. I didn't turn on the lights. There was a bar across the street, and the neon blinked first red, then green into the apartment. It was a nice mild spring night. I opened the windows, and I could hear the traffic noises on the Concourse. The apartment was very quiet.

I pulled an easy chair up to the window, and I lit a cigarette and sat smoking it, and then I got up and walked around the living room a while, and then I walked into the bedroom. The clock was ticking on the dresser, tick, tick, tick, tick. There was a framed picture of May alongside the clock, and there was her hairbrush on the dresser. I picked it up. Some of her black hair was still caught in it. I put it down quickly. I went back into the living room and stood by the window looking down at the street.

I was a big man.

I went to the telephone and dialed a number. I sat down and waited while it rang.

'Hello?' the voice said.

'Angelo, this is Frankie. Did I get you out of bed?'

'Oh, no Frankie,' he said. His voice was sleepy.

'Angelo, get in touch with Louise.'

'Yes, Frankie.'

'Send her up here right away.'

'Yes, Frankie.'

'Right away, you hear?'

'Yes, Frankie.'

'Good. And, Angelo – ' I heard the click on the line. I was a little disappointed. I guess I felt like talking to him a little. I guess so. And then, to tell the truth, I knew I really wanted to talk to May. I put her out of my mind. I began thinking of Louise instead. I lit another cigarette. I sat smoking for about a half-hour, thinking.

When the doorbell rang, I jumped. I turned in the chair and pulled out the new .45. For some reason, I began to sweat. All at once I thought of Andy and Weasel, and I thought of this new kid Georgie with the dollar signs in his eyes and the big fake grin on his mouth, and I began to sweat. My hand got so slippery I almost dropped the gun.

The doorbell rang again.

156

I went over to it. I threw off the safety catch on the .45. I leaned close to the door, listening. For just a second, I wondered how many damn doors I'd have to open in the years to come. And I wondered which one of them wouldn't open on a smiling honey blonde.

Trembling, I said, 'Who is it?'

FOR THE BEST IN PAPERBACKS, LOOK FOR THE

In every corner of the world, on every subject under the sun, Penguins represent quality and variety – the very best in publishing today.

For complete information about books available from Penguin and how to order them, write to us at the appropriate address below. Please note that for copyright reasons the selection of books varies from country to country.

In the United Kingdom: For a complete list of books available from Penguin in the U.K., please write to *Dept EP, Penguin Books Ltd, Harmondsworth, Middlesex, UB7 0DA*

In the United States: For a complete list of books available from Penguin in the U.S., please write to *Dept BA, Viking Penguin, 299 Murray Hill Parkway, East Rutherford, New Jersey 07073*

In Canada: For a complete list of books available from Penguin in Canada, please write to *Penguin Books Canada Limited, 2801 John Street, Markham, Ontario L3R 1D4*

In Australia: For a complete list of books available from Penguin in Australia, please write to the *Marketing Department, Penguin Books Australia Ltd, P.O. Box 257, Ringwood, Victoria 3134*

In New Zealand: For a complete list of books available from Penguin in New Zealand, please write to the *Marketing Department, Penguin Books (N.Z.) Ltd, Private Bag, Takapuna, Auckland 9*

In India: For a complete list of books available from Penguin in India, please write to *Penguin Overseas Ltd, 706 Eros Apartments, 56 Nehru Place, New Delhi 110019*

Also by Ed McBain in Penguins

'Ed McBain has terrific pace, an atmosphere of realism and smashing impact' – Erle Stanley Gardner

Cop Hater

Introducing Detective Steve Carella pitted against a ruthless cop killer.

The Mugger

Muggers snatch bags, and this one seems to be moving up into the murder bracket.

The Con Man

Teddy Carella, Steve's mute wife, runs a cold killer to earth.

The Pusher

Carella wrestles with the ugly activities of the dope traffickers.

Killer's Choice

Steve Carella investigates murder in a liquor store.

Lady Killer

An anonymous letter triggers off a manhunt in a city of eight million people.

Killer's Payoff

Detective Cotton Hawes tidies up the aftermath of a case of blackmail.

Killer's Wedge

A madwoman holds up the squadroom at gunpoint, bent on killing Carella.

'Til Death

Death is a guest in the aisles at the wedding of Steve Carella's sister.